THE GOLDEN ROAD DETOUR

By

Dona Bakker
and
Tami Riedeman

THE GOLDEN ROAD DETOUR

Copyright © 2008 Pastime Publications

Pastime Publications
1370 Trancas Street, #372
Napa, CA 94558
(707) 252-4062
www.napavalleypastime.com

or

KoodB Creations
P.O. Box 614
Sandstone, MN 55072
(320) 245-6949
koodbwriting.com

ISBN 10 – 09760276-5-8
ISBN 13 – 978-0-9760276-5-2

Cover Illustrations by Lauana Nelson, Cloquet, MN
lauana.nelson@gmail.com

Printed and Bound by Falcon Books, San Ramon, CA

Authors:
Dona Bakker and Tami Riedeman

The Golden Road Detour
is dedicated to
all souls who love to laugh.

In the beginning .....

Our first book, *The Golden Road, French Wine or Moonshine?"* told of the escapades of Grandy and Bernice, two female senior citizens with opposite personalities, become roommates at Passage of Time Retirement Home in the Twin Cities area of Minnesota. Not wanting to spend the rest of their lives eating Jell-O and playing bingo, the two fly to California to be on a game show. One of the ladies wins a motor home and soon afterwards Grandy and Bernice leave the retirement home and head off to visit the more unusual tourist sites of the United States (like the world's biggest Cheeto). Along the way they meet several characters who share in Grandy's obsession of UFO's and many others who just add entertainment to their adventures.

The trip is not all fun and games though, due to misunderstandings between the old women and the determination of a greedy son and ex-husband to catch up with one of the ladies. Believing his mother is mentally unstable and has more money than she professes, the son turns a leisurely trip into an exciting chase scene. The ending of the story leaves the reader wanting to find out what happens to these two zany friends. So here it is, the sequel to Grandy and Bernice's humor filled journey.

Chapter 1

"Bernice, tell Ditch to stop whimpering. I need to concentrate on my driving."

"It's not Ditch crying, Grandy, it's your grandson."

"What does he want?"

"I don't know, maybe it has something to do with us forgetting to give him back to his father," Bernice's voice was marinated in panic.

"Oh boy," Grandy said, "is Daddy Dakota going to be mad at me." The seventy year old grandma opened the motor home window to let in some fresh air. A blast of hot August wind stirred her multi-shaded red hair into a shape resembling runaway cotton candy. She seethed with resentment, blaming her eldest son, Avis and her no good ex-husband Lester for the predicament they had caused. If they hadn't decided to chase them all over the country, Grandy wouldn't be having memory lapses, especially concerning the return of her grandson, Rain to her middle son. The senior citizen settled on thoughts of how to get back at the two men who had been a major factor in trying to ruin her life. She smiled when the perfect idea invaded her thoughts.

In the back of the Fleetwood, Bernice tried to collect herself and quiet the blue-eyed infant. She offered him a pacifier which seemed to momentarily satisfy his needs. She then double checked to make sure his car seat was fastened securely. Grandy would never do anything to intentionally hurt anyone but her driving was not one of her more polished skills. Meanwhile, their nondescript dog Ditch found his rubber ball and dropped it at Bernice's feet.

"Not now Mutt," Bernice said sharply, "we have more important issues to be concerned about; like making a clean get away and finding a high quality beauty parlor where I can get my hair and nails done."

After an hour on the road, the silver-haired grandma walked an unsteady gait from the back of the motor home to the passenger seat. She looked warily at her best friend as she sat down. Grandy was completely absorbed in her driving and to interrupt her would probably invoke a spiky-tongued response.

"Grandy?"

"What?"

"Where are we going?"

"Somewhere to hide out."

"Can I call Joyce and see if she and the family made it to Texas?"

"No Bernie, they might be tracing our calls."

"I don't think Avis and Lester are worried about our phone calls right now, Grandy. They're probably busy trying to explain to the police why they're chasing after two old ladies. Besides, Dakota and your friend, Roscoe disabled their car."

The wild haired driver glanced over at her usually level headed traveling companion. Generally not one to show affection, Grandy offered a slight smile and said, "Bernie, you can call your daughter later. We're on a mission to find a place to hide out."

"Why don't we go to San Francisco? I'd love to see my sister, Charlotte; I haven't seen her in fifteen years. Nobody would think to look for us there."

"You told me she had Alzheimer's."

"That doesn't mean I don't want to see her. She might not be around much longer and it's important I see her." Bernice forced her grey eyes to tear up and gave Grandy a sad look.

"I swear Bernie, you ask for more pardons than a felon on death row. Either sit back and relax or go in the back and play with Ditch. It's important I watch for a secret hideout."

Resolved to the fact she wasn't getting anywhere with her requests, Bernice decided on a different approach.

"What about Rain? When are you going to call Dakota and make arrangements to meet?"

There was a long pause and a suspicious look thrown Bernice's direction. "Why are you in such a hurry to get rid of Rain?"

"I'm not in a hurry to get rid of him. I'm thinking poor Dakota is worried sick about him."

"Why? You don't think I take good care of my own flesh and blood?" Grandy's voice was sounding edgy.

"No, I didn't mean that, it's just –"

"Rain and Dakota are just fine. Besides, I think I need to look for a new mother for my grandson. His mother Skye can't possibly be a good mother if she's gone off on some stupid cause and left her baby behind. The woman should be fed to grizzly bears. No, I take that back. No reason to be unkind to the bears."

Bernice sighed and decided she was too tired for any more conversation. She stood up and started walking towards the back of the coach.

"Hang on, I'm making a sharp turn!" Grandy yelled. And as soon as the words left her mouth, she jerked the steering wheel to the left. Bernice grabbed at the nearest object to steady herself. Unfortunately, it was the refrigerator door which had not been properly locked. The door flew open, Bernice lost her balance, landed on her bottom and food exited the refrigerator at a high rate of speed. A rainbow of liquids and solids quickly covered the stunned traveler.

Chapter 2

Dakota watched in horror as his mother's Fleetwood left the Dairy Queen parking lot almost on two wheels. He couldn't believe that, even despite the commotion less than an hour ago, he and his son Rain had become separated. The frantic father ran his fingers through his long, dark hair and closed his indigo blue eyes for a silent prayer. He then called his mother's cell phone and heard only the voice mail.

"Ma, answer the phone! Where are you going? You still have Rain in the motor home. Ma! Answer the phone!" Dakota knew Grandy couldn't hear his pleas but it was all he could do for the moment.

"Don't worry Boy, your ma will take good care of your son," Roscoe said in a voice meant to sound comforting. The frantic father believed what the old hippy was saying but it still didn't make him feel better.

"They headed north, I should be able to catch up with them pretty easily," Dakota said. "Do you want to ride along Roscoe?"

"Nah, I like your mother, Dakota, but I think its better I sit this one out." Roscoe stroked his white beard and continued, "Every time I try to show your ma a bit of affection, she stomps on my feelings like a homemade grape press."

"Okay, well, thanks for your help today, I appreciate it."

"No problem."

After the two men shook hands and headed back to their respective vehicles, a couple of county sheriff deputies stopped them and requested a statement concerning the events that occurred right before Grandy and Bernice fled. Dakota tried to explain how important it was that he leave so he could catch up with his mother.

"This will only take a few minutes Mr. Wayland," the deputy said. "Now, tell me what happened."

4

Anxious to be on the road, Dakota decided to give the officer the short version of the chaos. Meanwhile, Roscoe took his time, embellishing a few details and providing elaborate gestures.

"It's like this Officer, my mother and her friend were attending an ISAET (I Saw an Extraterrestrial) meeting when my father and my older brother showed. They've been chasing after my ma for a few weeks now and finally caught up with her here. Because I knew she didn't want anything to do with them, Roscoe and I tried to convince them to leave her alone." Dakota's quick explanation left him breathless. He nervously looked at his vehicle.

"What do you know about your brother's car being disabled?" The deputy's voice was flat and because of his sunglasses, no emotion could be read in his eyes.

The young dad thought carefully before answering and hoped with all his might Roscoe was not giving a different story.

"I don't know who would have touched Avis' car; I was too busy trying to rescue my mother."

"What about your friend Roscoe? Do you think he could have sabotaged the vehicle?"

"I don't think so, he's Grandy's friend."

The pot bellied law enforcer said in a resigned voice, "Seems like EVERYBODY is Grandy's friend. Okay, thanks for your help Mr. Wayland, you can go now."

"Thank you, Officer." Dakota scurried to his pickup, started it up and headed north, this time praying out loud that it wouldn't take a miracle to get his son back.

* * * * *

Bernice would have yelled at her crazed friend but she didn't want to wake up Rain. Instead, she picked herself up off the floor and managed to make it to the bathroom. There the well-rounded grandma attempted to scrub orange juice, pureed blueberries and spaghetti sauce off her head, neck and face. After looking in the mirror, Bernice realized it was going to take a Brillo pad and several hot showers to remove the food remains from her skin. She shook her head in disgust, then went back into the bedroom to change her clothes. The outfit consisted of her favorite watermelon shorts, cherry red top and white sandals with red tassels. Because her hair still had faint traces of food stains, Bernice put a rainbow colored sun hat on her head. A couple of layers of red rose lipstick and the senior citizen was one step closer to feeling normal again. Bernice checked on Rain, then slowly made her way back to the front of the motor home just as it came to a stop.

"Grandy?"

"What?"

"Where are we?"

"At the place we're going to hide out for awhile."

"And where is that?"

"Santa Claus, California."

"Santa Claus? What kind of –"

"Bernie, you aren't starting to whine are you? You know how I feel about whining."

"No I'm not. I just –"

"Don't worry. This is a great place to hide out. Avis and Lester won't think to look here. Plus Rain can enjoy an early Christmas."

"Grandy, it's August, Rain is 2 months old and I bet this place doesn't have a decent beauty salon. I really need a salon, just look at my hair." Bernice whipped off her hat and bent her head close to her friend so she could see her hair disaster.

A low chuckle rumbled from Grandy. "Old Woman, you could take the fun out of a free trip to Disneyland. Rain and I are going to check this place out. You can stay here and pout, paint your nails or clean the toilet. I really don't care." And with that statement, Grandy unbuckled her seatbelt, went to the back of the motor home, picked up Rain and left.

A look of contempt clouded Bernice's face as she watched the two head towards a group of dilapidated buildings. She thought about following them but decided someone had to clean up the food mess off the floor.

Chapter 3

"Guess I underestimated your ma, Avis. Seems like she's got a few tricks in her handbag," Lester said in gruff irritation.

"Dad, I think it's better we both go home and forget about trying to catch up with her. I have a feeling it's going to be one big headache after another tracking her down and convincing her to return to the retirement home."

"We're not giving up, Son. Now that we know what she's driving and who she's with, it shouldn't be a problem."

Avis looked at his greasy-haired, pot-bellied father with resignation. How was he going to separate himself from the man who had as much compassion as a pebble in a laced-up hiking boot. While Lester belched and scratched himself, Avis called his wife at their home in St. Paul, Minnesota.

"Hey, Honey, it's me"

"Hi Avis, how's it going?" Liza's voice was low and out of breath.

"Are you okay? How come you're panting?" Avis could visualize his slender, face-like-a-model wife.

"I started a new exercise program today."

"Sounds like it's killing you. How's Augusta? Bet she was the star of the talent show."

Liza hesitated before answering, "Well, she was good, Honey, but I think we'll need to invest in some singing lessons for her."

Avis grimaced. "Oh. Sorry I missed the show. Next time I promise I'll be there."

"Did you catch up with your mother?"

"Almost. They got away."

"What do you mean got away? How fast can an old woman in a wheelchair go?"

"She's not in a wheelchair and it's complicated. I'll explain when I get home."

8

"Are you still going to try to find her?"

"Not right now, I need to think about this some more. I'm planning to take a flight home tomorrow. First I need to drop my dad off at his camper, just northwest of L.A."

"Is he still as nasty and smelly as always?"

Avis glanced at his dad and said softly, "Yes, I'm afraid so."

"Do NOT say hi for me and you had better not bring him home with you!"

"Not a problem, Dear. See you tomorrow."

"Sounds good. I've got to go now Honey, the noodles are getting cold. See you tomorrow."

"Noodles? What?" The sound of a disconnect was the only answer Avis heard. He stared a moment at the cell phone before hitting the end button.

"Everything alright at home?" Lester asked with a stupid grin on his face.

"Fine."

"What's that I heard about panting and noodles?" The old man's voice was starting to sound creepy.

"Nothing, Dad. I'm taking you to your pickup, then I'm going home. We'll deal with Mother later."

"Hey, Son?"

"What?"

"Say, I might just take a drive out to your place. Haven't seen my granddaughter in a while. Any chance I could crash on your couch for a short time? I can't go home."

"Why can't you go home?"

"My place is undergoing a remodeling and I need a place to plant my butt for awhile."

Avis gave his father a apprehensive look then asked, "What kind of remodeling?"

"Seems like my girlfriend wants a new model of a boyfriend. Hence, I've been tossed out on the street curb like a used pee-stained sofa."

"Dad, would love to help you out but I think I better just give you a few bucks so you can find your own place. Right now I need a break from you and Ma."

Chapter 4

With the warm air and the light of a full moon reflecting off the Pacific Ocean, Grandy didn't realize it was nearly midnight. She walked with Rain past several rundown, deserted businesses including a derailed miniature train station and a merry-go-round held hostage by weeds. Just when she was about to admit defeat (a rare occurrence for the old redhead), she saw a half-lit building with the name *Santa's Kitchen* on it. A worn sign advertised good food and family fun. Christmas lights with half of them burnt out hung haphazardly over the porch rail and plastic reindeer, chipped and faded, lay propped up next to the front door.

"Just great," mumbled Grandy, "It looks like Santa fell off the roof and landed on hard times." She hugged Rain a little tighter and walked inside.

At first, the low lighting disguised the tired decor of the establishment. Upon closer inspection, it was evident the spirit of the holidays had been abandoned by those working year 'round in the town of Santa Claus. Drab artificial pine trees, boxes wrapped in Christmas paper, and silver tinsel had all become stripped of brightness and wholeness. A woman dressed in a matted fake fur, shiny velvet Santa's helper suit approached Grandy.

"Hi, my name is Bobbie, and I'll be your server tonight." The dark haired woman with brown eyes was genuine in her greeting yet lacked a full pot of cheeriness.

"My name's Grandy McGregor, and I brought my grandson, Rain, to see Santa Claus."

Bobbie glanced at the baby then replied apologetically, "I'm sorry, but Santa left for vacation yesterday. The closest thing we have to St. Nick is him," and she pointed to the bartender in the corner.

"Fine. I'll come by again in December. How about some food? We're hungry," Grandy said in her sandpaper voice.

"We stopped serving dinner at 10:00 p.m., I could probably find something in the freezer and heat it up in the microwave."

"I'd settle for stale pretzels and soggy peanuts, but my grandson needs something with more substance."

"How about warm milk for the cute one and mini corn dogs and tacos for you?"

"Here's his bottle and make sure you bring lots of ketchup for the other stuff."

"You got it, Grandy," Bobbie winked at her newest customers and retreated to the kitchen.

"Well, Rain? Does she seem like mommy material to you? The outside package is fine so far. Let's quiz her and see what substance she has on the inside."

Twenty minutes later, Bobbie filled Grandy's table with the food, including a couple of molasses cookies decorated with stiff frosting. "This is far from gourmet, but it will fill your tummy. By the way, who named your grandson Rain? It's an interesting name."

"His dad, my son, Dakota, did. Here, feed him his bottle while I eat. Doesn't look like you have any other customers to worry about."

"No," Bobbie said, a wisp of sadness in her voice, "only old Clarence sitting at the bar. He's here every night and has become a fixture of the decor in this place. Nice guy, but never seems to have quite enough change for even the smallest tip." There was a slight pause before Bobbie tentatively asked, "Where is Rain's mom and dad?"

"Dakota is somewhere farther south of here duking it out with my ex-husband and other son, and Rain's so-called mother, Skye, is off somewhere braiding daisy chains or some other dumb thing."

Grandy stuffed her mouth with food, then began launching more questions at Bobbie. "How come this town is so dead? Why are you still working here? Where did Santa go on vacation? What do you think about UFO's? Where did you get the name Bobbie? Were you supposed to be a boy? Do you have a husband or boyfriend?"

The young waitress didn't know whether to laugh or feel insulted by this most unusual senior citizen. Meanwhile, Rain lay content in her arms unaware of his grandma's search for a new mother for him.

"Well, I'm not sure what caused the town of Santa Claus to become so crippled. I'm sure it's a combination of economy and competition from newer and bigger attractions. Some guy bought the land in 1943 after he almost died of a heart attack, turned it into Christmas all year round – rides for the kids, and rows of Christmas stores. It used to be really fun. All that's left now is a souvenir shop and us. As for why I'm still working here," Bobbie paused and looked at Rain, "I still believe in the magic of Christmas."

Grandy swallowed half a glass of eggnog, belched, then asked, "What about the answers to my other questions?"

"Santa Claus is vacationing somewhere in South America, I don't know if I believe in UFO's, Bobbie is short for Roberta, I'm sure I wasn't supposed to be a boy, and finally, I was married for a short time."

"What happened?"

"I caught him wrapping one of Santa's helpers."

Grandy scrutinized Bobbie a moment before saying, "I'll be right back."

"Where are you going?"

"To talk to the bartender. What's his name?"

"Bert."

The bewildered waitress watched Grandy hobble up to the bar and begin a conversation with Bert.

"Tell me about Bobbie. Does she have any baggage?"

"Everybody has baggage, why are you asking?" He eyed the old lady with distrust.

"I mean the big stuff; like a rap sheet, crazy relatives, or watches *The Price is Right* everyday?"

"Bobbie is a sweetheart and I watch out for her, if you know what I mean," Bert gave Grandy a look that was intended to be a warning. Unfortunately, his round face and Santa hat only made him look like a distorted overgrown elf.

Bobbie looked confused as her red-headed customer returned and took Rain out of her arms.

"Something wrong, Grandy?"

"No. I need your phone number though, in case it doesn't work out."

"In case what doesn't work out?"

"Skye and Dakota. I think Rain may be needing a new mother and you might just work."

At first, Bobbie didn't think she heard Grandy correctly. But after seeing Bert roll his eyes and recalling the questions she had been asked, there was no doubt in her mind that the old lady was completely sincere in her quest.

* * * * *

Grandy and Rain returned to the motor home to find Bernice scrubbing the toilet.

"Okay, What's the matter now? You only scrub the toilet in the middle of the night when something's bugging you. What'd you do, break a nail?"

"Well,... um... No, I turned your phone on to listen to the messages."

"You what?"

"I just wanted to see if Joyce called. Anyway, the phone rang and I answered it."

"You what? Oh, great! Now we're gonna have to change course again. Who was it?"

"It was Dakota."

"Where is he, and what did you tell him?"

"I remember you telling me the phone might be bugged, so I told him I didn't know where we were. He's really worried about Rain, Grandy. I told him you'd call him in the morning.
Grandy then mumbled something unintelligible and handed Rain to Bernice. "He's wet. I'm going to bed."

Bernice stood in the livingroom holding Rain. "Your grandma's a little upset. We better not bother her right now." As she dug around in the baby's bag for a diaper, a napkin fell out with writing on it.

"What's this Rain?" She read the name Bobbie and a phone number next to it. "I hope this isn't another delirious space alien freak your grandmother met. We don't need any more weird people in our lives, do we Rain?" Bernie hummed softly to the sleepy baby while, in the background, Grandy snored like a jacked up 4x4 without a muffler.

Chapter 5

Bernice was awakened at 6 a.m. by Rain's demand for some breakfast. She rubbed her tired eyes and looked at the crying baby. Two-hour increments of sleep was for new mothers, not for a woman who sometimes wears diapers herself. Just as Rain's wailing reached a crescendo, so did Grandy's singing in the shower. Ditch didn't want to miss the concert, so he began to howl in unison with the occupants of the motor home. Bernice put a bottle in the microwave and turned on the coffee maker. The sight of the worn remnants of Santa Claus town was even more dismal in the morning light. A deep sadness overwhelmed Bernice as she thought of her daughter and granddaughter in Texas and her recent role of babysitter for a baby that was not related to her. From somewhere she didn't know existed, Bernice hollered, "Grandy!"

"What!"

"Get out here and take care of Rain and Ditch, I want to–" Bernice stopped herself before finishing the sentence. Her plan was to demand her psycho friend take her to civilization so she could go to church. Then she remembered the nightmare the last time she and Grandy went. Chanting while sitting cross legged on a dirty wooden floor was not Bernice's idea of worship.

"You want to what?" said the irritated, wet-haired grandma.

Bernice's eyes became wide as tennis balls as she observed her friend's new appearance. It was apparent Grandy was not about to give up her trademark red hair, but she had found a new shade unlike anything her plain Jane roommate had ever seen.

"What did you do to your hair?" gasped Bernice.

"That's a dumb question, I colored it."

"I know that. But what's the name of the shade you used? It looks weird."

" Hey, you should talk. Your hair looks like a cotton ball rolled in ashes. And if you must know, the name of my shade is Neon Burgundy."

"Well, I can't believe anybody makes that color."

"Nobody does, I mixed it up myself. Now, what was it you wanted?"

"Nothing. Hurry up, get dressed, and take care of your family. I'm anxious to see Charlotte."

"Turn your fire down, Bernie. I have to make a quick call to Dakota first. Rain is crying, feed him his bottle and feed Ditch while you're at it."

Bernice did not want to engage in another battle with her traveling companion, so she silently started followed Grandy's demands. Wrapped in a Star Trek bath towel, the redhead sat at the dinette table and called her son.

* * * * *

"Hello. Ma! Where are you?! Why didn't you answer your cell phone earlier? Is Rain okay? I've-"

"Dakota, close that jaw of yours for one minute, will ya? You know our phone calls are being listened in on and we can't reveal too much information. Plus they can find us by tracing the calls."

"Ma, you listen to me and listen real carefully. I promise you that nobody is listening to our conversation. Lester and Avis do not know where you are and anything you say is-"

"I found a mother for Rain."

The switch in conversation startled the young man and he was silent for a moment before replying. "You what? What do you mean you found a mother for Rain? He already has one. Skye is his mother, remember? And I would really like to get him back so we can go see her."

"Skye is a horrible mother. How can anybody go off and leave their defenseless baby? I found a better one for him."

17

"Ma, I love you very much but I'm losing patience with you. Skye is a great mother and someday I will explain it all to you. Now, where are we going to meet so I can pick up my son?"

Grandy closed her eyes to think about the best place for a rendezvous.

"Ma?"

"Hush, boy, I'm thinking."

Another minute went by before Grandy said, "I got it. Tomorrow morning you call Chet Baxter at K-TAZ radio. He'll have the name of the place where we can meet and when."

"This makes no sense, Ma. Just tell me where you're headed."

"Can't do it over the phone right now, don't have my transmission protection outfit on. See you soon."

"But – " Silence at the other end of the phone signaled Grandy was done with the conversation and it would do no good to call back. Dakota knew the phone would be shut off. The young father banged his head against the palm of his hand while muttering creative profanities.

Chapter 6

The drive to San Francisco was turning out to be long and boring for Grandy, Bernice, Rain, and Ditch. So far, there had been no garage sales to stop at and no unusual sites to visit. The red-headed grandma kept hitting the search button on the radio trying to find a UFO talk show.

Bernice spoke quietly and politely to Grandy, "Why don't you try finding a Country Western station? We could all use a good sing-a-long."

"You don't like Country music, how come the sudden change?" Grandy's asked.

"I would rather listen to the twang of a guitar than the constant static of you switching stations."

Grandy changed the subject. "How is Rain? Does he need to be fed? Why don't you give Ditch a bath in some of your Jean Nate shower gel, he's starting to smell a little ripe."

"Rain's fine. I just changed and fed him. And you give your own darn dog a bath and use whatever stinking stuff you own. Leave my Jean Nate alone. Now, when are we getting to San Francisco? Will it be too late to go to Charlotte's? Can we – "

"Bernie, sounds like your bra straps are too tight. Close your mouth, we'll be there when we get there." Grandy gave her annoyed friend the hand sign for "go away."

Without another word of argument, Bernice walked towards the motor home bedroom. She glanced at Rain sleeping peacefully in his car seat. "You poor child," she sighed, "hope your grandma catches the nice bug before you get too much older."

* * * * *

A red sun was sliding into the ocean as the threesome entered the city of San Francisco. Grandy was demanding Bernice give her the easiest directions on how to get to Charlotte's nursing home.

"But I don't remember how to get around, its been years since I've been here and things have changed," whimpered Bernice. "Pull into a gas station, maybe they can help us."

Grandy would have preferred to skip the visit to see Bernice's sister. She thought taking the motor home down Nob Hill would be a lot more fun. So would making the Fleetwood jump the hills like the cars on T.V. cop shows. Bernice's pleading won out though and Old Red pulled into a service station for directions.

* * * * *

It was another two hours before the ladies found the Bayside Nursing Home. Grandy had insisted on driving over then back across the Golden Gate Bridge, twice. Bernice tried to calm her anger by dividing her time between caring for Rain and primping to see her sister. She had found a purple paisley top and matching skirt to wear. Fussing with her hair seemed like a moot point. It had been way too long since she had seen a professional stylist. Trying to salvage some vanity, Bernice painted her fingernails a strawberry pink and applied matching lipstick.

"Okay, Bernie, we're here. Hurry up and see Charlotte so we can go find a decent place to eat, I'm hungry."

"Aren't you going with me to meet my sister?"

"Nah, I hate retirement homes, they smell like leftover sauerkraut in a hot van."

"I'm not sure how long I'll be. I haven't seen Charlotte in a really long time."

"I'll give you half an hour, then I'm leaving."

"Half an hour! That's not enough time, Grandy! I don't know what room she's in or how to get to it."

"Fine. Take an hour then. But don't be late!"

The look Bernice gave Grandy was one of total contempt. She tried her best to stomp down the steps of the motor home but she almost tripped instead.

Fifteen minutes after Bernice left, she was back in the coach.

"That was fast Bernie, did Charlotte throw you out because of your outfit?" Grandy snickered.

"Not funny, Old Woman," Bernice snapped back. "Charlotte has been moved to the Bayside Extended Living Apartments. Apparently, she was misdiagnosed and doesn't have Alzheimer's after all."

"Well, that puts a burp in your bell doesn't it? If she doesn't have Alzheimer's, then why hasn't she contacted you all these years?"

"I don't know. Maybe she's mad because I didn't come visit her more often. Or maybe she forgot she has a sister. I don't know, Grandy, but we need to go see her. I got the directions from one of the nurses inside."

"Since your long lost sister is not on her death bed, let's go eat. I'm starved."

"I can't think of food at a time like this, we need to go find her."

"Okay, but I'm just going to drop your highnee off and you can visit while me and Rain go get something to eat."

"Fine. Let's just get going."

True to Grandy's words, she dropped her friend off at the retirement home and sped off to find some authentic Chinese food. Bernice watched the Fleetwood cut in front of vehicles and almost run over a pedestrian.

"Lord Almighty," said Bernice with a shake of her head, "that senior citizen is going to get in an accident yet." She turned and walked towards her sister's home.

Chapter 7

Standing before the pink stucco retirement home, Bernice paused to admire its simple Spanish style entrance and desert style landscape. Despite the beauty of the place, a knot formed in her stomach. It was only a few short months ago that she and Grandy had been living at *"The Passage of Time"* retirement home in Minnesota. Vowing never to return to its rubber ball tasting food and boring activities, Bernice still feared ending up back there.

Once inside the building, Bernice stopped at the restroom to compose herself, checking her makeup, and stuffing toilet paper under her armpits to keep the perspiration from staining her blouse. She felt the eyes of an elderly man follow her as she hobbled towards the front desk. His toothy grin reminded her of Leisure Suit Larry, a perverted retirement home resident back home.

In a bright and airy sitting area near the entrance, an old lady was slumped forward in her chair in front of a blaring television. "That old woman resembles Stella," Bernice thought to herself, "I wonder if she ever got new hearing aids?" Suddenly feeling younger than those around her, Bernice straightened her back and increased the speed of her pace. At the front desk she said in a polite but firm voice, "Excuse me, I'm looking for Charlotte Walker's room."

The middle-aged receptionist whose name tag said, "Hannah," cocked her head at the almost familiar looking woman standing in front of her.

"Charlotte Walker? May I ask who you are?"

"Bernice Gibson, her sister."

Hannah pushed her black rimmed glasses farther up her nose bridge and stared at the senior citizen a moment before exclaiming, "Oh yes! Bernice! I've heard Char mention your name many times. Come to think of it, you do look a little bit like her. Welcome to San Francisco!"

"Thank you. Char? You call her Char?"

"Everybody calls her Char. She insists the name Charlotte sounds too old fashioned."

A puzzled Bernice continued, "I hope my visit won't be a hardship on my sister."

"Hardship? Mercy sakes, Bernice. If anything, you might be suffering the hardship. It's a wonder anyone can keep up with your sister."

Bernice gave the nurse an inquisitive look. "Are you sure we're talking about the same person? I haven't seen my sister in almost 15 years and she is quite a bit older than me. I -"

"Yes, it's a shame the two of you haven't visited before now. You'll have a lot to catch up on."

"I'm sure Charlotte won't remember me, especially with her condition and all."

"Don't be silly! Of course she'll remember you! Just follow the hallway in front of you all the way to the end. Go out the double doors and you should see Char and about seven others in a yoga class."

By now Bernice was thoroughly confused and decided it would be easier to see for herself the woman Hannah was referring to as her sister. Once outside, she scanned the small yoga group and was shocked almost to the point of hyperventilation. There she saw a slender, much more youthful Charlotte, sitting in a semi-lotus position on a mat near the front of the class. As Bernice watched her sibling and the others follow the teacher's commands, her mind was torpedoed with several scenarios. One, this really wasn't Charlotte, just a look-a-like. Two, her sister discovered a secret age-reversing potion (which Bernice intended to get her hands on.) Or three, Bernice was experiencing some Twilight Zone episode that Grandy had somehow orchestrated.

Five minutes later, the yoga class ended. As Char rolled up her mat, Bernice approached, with caution, not sure whether she really wanted this woman to be her sister or not.

Char caught her sister's eye. "Bernice!?" She pounced over to her sibling and gave her a big hug. "I can't believe it's really you!"

"Charlotte! What happened to you? I thought you had Alzheimer's?"

The white haired 82 year old laughed, then abruptly stopped. "I was misdiagnosed. Then I had a reaction to some of the medication they had me on. I quit taking everything except my vitamins, minerals, enzymes, omegas, herbals and homeopathics. Now I feel 30 years younger and look 20 years younger. At least that's what I've been told by the men living down the hallway. Char winked before giving her sister another hug. "Why didn't you ever come and visit me, Bernice? What kept you away so long?"

The younger sister's face turned a deep shade of red and she closed her eyes in shame. "I'm so sorry, Charlotte, the last few times I saw you, you didn't even know who I was. It was too painful to continue visiting all the way from Minnesota. Then Jack died, and before I knew it, I was out traveling the countryside with my friend Grandy.

"I see," Charlotte's voice was a soft affirmation.

"Charlotte?"

"Yes."

"Why didn't you call me after you got better."

It was Charlotte's turn to be embarrassed. "I tried to call your number but it was disconnected. I didn't know how to find you after that."

The sisters looked sheepishly at one another and embraced once more in a heartfelt hug.

"Let's go back to my room, Bernice. I want to hear all about what's happened in your life these last 15 years."

In room 319, Bernice sat down as Charlotte busied herself in the kitchen. "Cup of green tea?"

"Uh, sure. I can't believe how great you look. But tell me why you want people to call you Char? You used to hate that name when you were younger."

"Thanks for the compliment. Many things have changed for me, Bernice. Char sounds more 'today.' But let's talk about what's been happening with you. How is Joyce? Is she married? Has she made you a grandma yet? Tell me all about your trip?"

"Joyce lives in Texas with her wonderful husband, Buck, and I have the world's most beautiful granddaughter."

"What's her name?"

"Jackie, after her grandpa Jack."

"Good for her. I sure enjoyed it when you brought Joycie to visit when she was little. It made up for not having any kids of my own. I got to spoil her."

"And that you did. As did her father."

The sisters continued to chat nonstop as an entire pot of green tea and a plateful of homemade oatmeal cookies slowly vanished. When it seemed like all the major and minor topics had been discussed, Bernice asked Charlotte, "Are you happy here?"

"Sometimes. But I just feel I've been given a new lease on life and I feel restless. You know, Rich and I had plans to travel after he retired, but then he up and died, and I was lost without him. Then I got sick, went through a long recovery and here I am, more money than I know what to do with. My friends are either dead or too old to do anything or go anywhere."

"I've got a great idea!"

"What's that?"

"Maybe you could go with me and Grandy. We've had such a great time, and oh the sites we've seen! We even went to a rodeo, if you can believe it."

"A rodeo? You?"

"Yeah, I know. I've done a lot of things in the last couple of months you wouldn't believe. Grandy is such an adventurer. She's been good for me. Otherwise I'd just be sitting in that old retirement home crocheting potholders and watching endless reruns of 'Little House on the Prairie.' You should come with us."

"What about Grandy? You think she'll go for it?"

"Hey, she kinda owes me. Between Ditch, and April and Rain..."

"Huh?"

"More long stories. Someday I'll tell you all about them. What do you say?"

"Well, let's check with Grandy first. Then I'll decide. I haven't even met her."

"She's a little different, but she kinda grows on you after a while."

"What do you mean 'different?'"

"Well, try to imagine a marriage of Lucille Ball and ET."

Chapter 8

It was late at night when Grandy marched into the retirement home with Rain cradled in one arm and Ditch tucked under the other.

"What room is Charlotte in?" she demanded from Hannah.

"Charlotte who? And who are you?" The receptionist was instantly on alert.

"Charlotte is Bernice's sister, and I'm Grandy."

"One moment, please." Hannah picked up the phone and dialed Charlotte's extension. She turned her face and spoke quietly, "Char, this is Hannah. There is a woman with a baby, a dog and a hair color that should be outlawed wanting to know where your room is. She said her name is Grandy."

"You can send her to my room, Hannah, she's harmless."

"Are you sure? She seems a little strange."

"It'll be fine."

Okay. What about the dog?"

"Let her bring the dog. It won't be worth the hassle to tell her otherwise."

"Whatever you say, Char." Hannah hung up the phone and spoke to Grandy in her professional manner.

"Take the hallway in front of you down halfway, make a left-hand turn, and Char's room will on the right hand side. Number 319."

"Thanks."

* * * * *

The door to Char's room stood open by the time Grandy arrived. She walked right in, placed Ditch on Bernice's lap, and nodded her head towards Char.

"Grandy," Bernice said, "This is my sister, Char. Char, this is Grandy, Rain, and Ditch." Bernice tried to smile with sincerity as she held the restless dog in her lap.

"Nice to meet you, Grandy. Bernice has told all about your fun trip."

"I think it's been fun. Your sister, here, belly aches a lot." Grandy licked her fingers and ran them across the plate where the cookies had been. The small crumbs on her fingers fell off and sprinkled down the front of her denim shirt.

A look of amusement spread over Char's face and she patted Grandy on the back. "I should kick your butt for talking about my sister like that, except I know she can be that way sometimes."

"Charlotte!" A mortified Bernice exclaimed, "How can you say that about me!"

"Because it's true, Bernie," Grandy replied. "We need to get going, give your sister a hug so we can leave."

"Uh, Grandy?"

"What?"

"Do you think Char could travel with us for awhile? She has money to help pay for gas and she likes dogs and babies." Bernice thrust Ditch into her sister's arms. "See?"

"It gets too crowded with three people in the motor home," Grandy said.

"It wasn't too crowded with April in the motor home. Grandy, pleeeassse, She doesn't take up much space."

"You don't have any creepy hobbies or anything, do you, Charlie?"

"Not unless you consider an interest in the history of pyramids creepy?"

Bernice's eyes bulged as she looked at her sister with surprise.

"Char! You didn't mention you liked pyramids!"

"Guess I forgot to mention that one, Sis. We ran out of time to discuss *everything*. By the way, I find mummies rather interesting, too."

Grandy decided that, although she had only known the elder of the two sisters for a few minutes, she figured that Char might be okay, especially if she liked mummies and teasing Bernice.

"Fine, Charlie can go with us. She can get her stuff together while we set up camp for the night," said Grandy.

"What RV park are you staying at?" asked Char.

"We're not. We're parked in the parking lot."

"I'm not sure you can do that," Char remarked.

"Yes, she can," replied Bernice, "Grandy pretty much does what she wants."

Chapter 9

"Good morning, and Happy Monday! Welcome to the Chet Baxter Show. I'm your host, Chet Baxter, with another three hours of lively entertainment from Chicago. I'm happy to announce, we have several new stations just added to our listening audience. We are now syndicated in over 150 cities across the United States. Before Grandy and Bernice call in, I thought I'd better fill our new listeners in on our traveling grandmas. Throughout the year, I broadcast my show from different, unusual events across the United States. During my travels this summer, I met the most extraordinary women, two sassy seniors, Grandy and Bernice, who are traveling across the country in a motor home they won on the *Price is Right*. Their story so intrigued me, and their interactions so entertaining, I invited them to be on my show, every weekday morning at this time. They call in and report on their travels and experiences on the road. In a few short weeks, they have amassed quite a following, with fan clubs popping up in every city. You, the listeners, are given an opportunity to call in and talk personally to Bernice and Grandy, ask them anything you want. That has been quite entertaining, as well. I think we have them on the line right now. Ladies, are you there?"

"Good morning, Chet.," said Bernice is a sappy sweet voice.

"Good morning, Bernice. How are you and Grandy this fine day?"

"Just wonderful, Chet! I've been visiting with my sister, Charlotte, who I haven't seen in a really long time!"

"Well, how awesome for you and Charlotte!"

"Yes, and she is going to travel with me and Grandy!"

"That is very exciting, Bernice! Speaking of Grandy, is she there? I'd like to say hi to her, too."

Bernice paused before saying softly, "Yeah, she's here, but she's sort of, cranky."

"I am not!" hollered Grandy in the background. She grabbed the cell phone from her prissy companion and said tartly, "I'm not cranky, Bernie just always finds a way to put a hole in my happy balloon."

"Well, good morning, Grandy," Chet said with a big smile on his face, "why don't you tell us all about your latest travel adventures."

"You know I can't reveal too much, my no-good ex-husband and son are still looking for me. I can tell you I met a woman I think would be a good mom for my grandson, and I'm anxious to leave this town, too many weirdos."

"Okay, anything else you want to tell your listening audience before I open it up to phone calls?"

"No, but if my son Dakota is listening, he needs to call in, I have a message to give him."

"Sure thing, Grandy. Now, we have Zeke from Scottsdale, Arizona on the line. Go ahead, Zeke."

"Hey Grandy, I've been listening to yours and Bernice's travel stories for the last couple of months. I was wondering if the two of you plan to visit Arizona anytime soon. I have this castle I built all by myself out of dried alien bones I found in the desert. And I'd like you to see it."

"You're a liar, Zeke."

"What!"

"I said, you're a liar, you couldn't have made a castle out of dried alien bones. When aliens die their bones dissolve and become meteors in space."

There was a loud click that echoed through the air waves when Zeke hung up and a small teacup of silence before Chet tried to rescue the awkward moment.

"Well, that was certainly an interesting conversation."

"Chet."

"Yes, Grandy."

"No more calls from perverts."

"Well, you're in luck, Grandy, we have your son, Dakota, on the line. Do you want to take any more calls from your fan club first?"

"No."

"Okay then," Chet's voice detected a trace of awkwardness.

"I need to talk to Dakota off the air."

"Okay. Ladies and gentlemen, sounds like Grandy has an important family matter to take care of. We'll talk with you and Bernice tomorrow, right Grandy?"

"Yeah, sure, just put Dakota through and shut off the mike, or whatever it is you do. Don't want anybody listening in."

"Do you want to say good-bye to your listening audience first?"

"No."

"Okay Grandy, you're off the air. Here's Dakota and we'll talk to you tomorrow."

"Ma, what is going on?"

"You can pick up Rain tomorrow at 2 p.m. at Alcatraz."

"Alcatraz?"

"The prison. San Francisco."

"Why can't we meet at a restaurant or rest area?"

"Not safe enough, Son."

"Ma, I really don't think Dad or Avis are still following you."

"Can't be sure, Dakota. Just be at Alcatraz tomorrow." Grandy hung up the phone.

"Alcatraz?" Bernice asked.

"They'll never find us there."

"Wait a minute. I remember the last time you took me to a prison. I sure don't want to relive that nightmare."

"You exaggerate, Bernie, it wasn't that bad."

"That's your opinion. I think Char and I will go get our hair and nails done. You and Rain can meet Dakota at Alcatraz."

"While you're out running around, find a place to get Ditch bathed. He's starting to smell like a dog."

Bernice rolled her eyes while muttering, "he is a dog, you old bag, and I'm NOT taking him into the beauty parlor with me."

Chapter 10

Dakota desperately wished his car could attain the speed of a flying saucer. Because he didn't know where his mother, Bernice and Rain had stopped for the night, he was several hours behind them. Dakota missed Rain and the young father was not looking forward to explaining to his wife that their baby was on the lam with his eccentric mother. And what was the deal with meeting Grandy at Alcatraz? Dakota understood his mother far better than his two brothers, yet there were times when even he had to admit her behavior exceeded the unusual.

* * * * *

"Grandy, I highly recommend you take a cable car to the pier. Trying to deal with the traffic and parking your motor home in San Francisco is no easy feat," said Charlotte.

"Well, if it wasn't for those crazy cable car drivers clanging their bells at me, I'd be just fine."

"I suppose you cut right in front of them, didn't you? Bernice remarked sarcastically.

Grandy snapped back, "No! I don't know what their problem was. I motioned with my hand for them to go around me but they chose not to."

Char snickered softly.

"What's so funny?" said an irritated Grandy.

"Cable cars run on tracks, Grandy. They can't maneuver like a motor vehicle."

Grandy gave Charlotte and Bernice a disgusted look, turned away and began getting Rain ready to go meet his dad. Trying to avoid an unpleasant flare-up, Bernice asked Grandy in a most respectful tone of voice about the daily phone call to Chet.

"You call him and mention that we're headed to a new attraction called *"Alice in Wonderland."* When he asks where that is, tell him it's a place where there's a lot of fruits and nuts."

"What if he asks for a specific location or what kind of rides it has?" Worry was slowly crawling into Bernice's voice.

"Use your imagination, Bernie. You do have one, don't you?"

"Of course I do!"

"Okay Ladies, let's concentrate on the tasks at hand," Charlotte said in calm voice. "Bernice, let's head down the hallway to the beauty shop. Grandy needs to finish her preparations."

"I'm leaving Ditch here. He'll get seasick on the boat to Alcatraz. Don't forget to take him out for potty breaks. And remember to feed and water him."

Bernice was instantly angered by her traveling companion's constant demands. She said tersely, "If that mutt was going to get seasick, he would have done it while you drove. And why do I always have to take care of him? He's your dog."

"Hey, I agreed to take your sister along when we go back on the road. How do I know she won't be more trouble than one small dog? Besides, you like Ditch. You just pretend you don't."

Charlotte watched with amusement as the two old ladies continued to banter back and forth. Despite the snide remarks and snippy voice tones, it was evident the two women liked each other, even if they pretended they didn't. It was time though, to change the current course of conversation.

"If I become too much of a bother, Grandy, you can put me and Bernice on a plane to Paris."

"Oh Char!" Bernice clapped her hands and exclaimed, "that would be just heaven! I've always wanted to go to Paris! You know-"

"Now look what you started, Charlie," Grandy said in frustration. "Never tell your sister you might do this or that. She'll drive you crazy until it happens. On our trip out here she must have asked four thousand times, 'are we there yet?' Just like some impatient little kid."

Rather than start another bickering session, Bernice ignored Grandy, picked up Rain, kissed the infant and whispered to him, "Hope to see you again soon, Little Man. Don't let your grandma drop you overboard."

Chapter 11

A groggy voice answered the phone, "Yeah?"

"Who is this?" asked Avis.

"Z. Who is this?"

"Avis, Howard's brother. Who are you?"

"Blackie's brother. Heard a lot about you, Man? How was California?"

"Fine," said Avis in an annoyed tone, "can I speak to Howard?"

"Sure, Man." Z turned his head slightly and shouted, "Howard! Your bro's on the phone!" He spoke again to Avis, "He'll be right here, nice talking to ya, Man."

"Same here," Avis said flatly.

"Hey Avis! How's the big sunny C?" the younger brother said in mock enthusiasm.

"Didn't go as planned. Have you heard from Mom?"

"No. She's probably been too busy running from you. Why don't you give her a break? She's a bit crazy, but she's harmless."

"Crazy? That's an understatement. She and that roommate of hers almost cost me and Dad a night in jail. I think every mile she travels she gets a bit more unbalanced. I have a couple of ideas on how I can finally catch up with her. I've decided to take a vacation with the family first, let Mom get the impression I've given up the chase."

In his mind, Howard could clearly see his older brother's expression. His green eyes would be gleaming with the confidence of conquest and his hand smoothing over the fading strands of brown and silver hair. It was futile to engage in a conversation in the defense of their mother, so he decided to end the phone call.

"Well, I need to go, Avis. Blackie's decided she's ready to start a family and she's says now's the time to drink the liquids and eat the foods of the fertility gods."

"Your wife is a spoke of the weird wheel, just like Mom. Be careful Howard, you might be conducting your own search someday. And speaking of Blackie, what is her brother doing at your house? I thought he was in jail."

"Z got out yesterday. He's only staying a couple of days while his new apartment is being painted."

"Watch your back. Most criminals don't rehabilitate."

"Not to worry. Z is not exactly the smartest convict. His petty theft passion was stealing the sunflower seeds from his neighbor's bird feeders and the lawn ornaments from his yard."

"That doesn't sound like an offense the courts would incarcerate him for."

"Yeah well, his neighbor was the deputy district attorney." There was a micro pause before Howard continued, "Really Avis, I gotta go. Blackie's waiting for me."

"Fine. Go drink your nectar and eat your cupcakes. But I'm sure the world would agree that the offspring produced from your wife would not exactly be a benefit to society."

A dial tone was the only response Avis heard to his undignified comment. He shrugged his shoulders then put in a call to his travel agent.

"Hello. Around the World Travel. This is Sean."

"Sean. Avis Wayland. I need three round trip tickets to Hawaii, five nights stay in Maui and a rental car."

"How are you doing, Mr. Wayland? Nice to hear from you again. When do you want to leave for Hawaii?"

"Doing fine and make it for Friday."

"This Friday?"

"Yes, this Friday. Call me at my office when you have the arrangements made."

"Of course, Mr. Wayland? Anything else I can help you with?"

"Yeah. Make sure the room has double sinks and doesn't have any yellow on the wallpaper."

"No yellow wallpaper?" Sean sounded a bit confused.

"You heard right. No yellow wallpaper. My wife hates the color yellow and especially despises it in wallpaper. It reminds her of mustard and she really can't stand mustard."

"Not a problem, Mr. Wayland. I'll call you when I'm done making the arrangements."

When Avis had hung up, Sean shook his head and muttered to himself, "Now that is one very strange family."

Chapter 12

Grandy inquired at the front desk where to catch the cable car, only to discover there was no cable car link anywhere close by. If time had been her friend, she would have gone back to the beauty shop and told Bernice what a stupid sister she had. Instead, she walked outside, stood next to the motor home and pondered her next move.

"Well, Rain, trying to park this monster might be a bit tricky. I guess Charlie was right." Grandy turned and went back inside to call a cab, which arrived within minutes.

"Alcatraz, and hurry," Grandy barked at the cabbie.

"I take you to ferry, ferry take you to island."

"Do you have a brother named Habib?"

"Pardon?"

"Never mind, just drive." Grandy gazed into Rain's blue eyes. "Thank heaven you look like me and not your grandfather. That no good son of a garbage disposal better not still be following us, or I'll make sure he becomes an appetizer for the San Francisco bay sharks."

The cabbie glanced at his patron through the mirror. "Is someone following you? You hang on back there. I lose them." His driving became erratic as he wove in and out of traffic, jerking Grandy and her grandson back and forth across the backseat.

"You better slow down, Habib, before I introduce you to my heavy weight champion purse. No one's following us. Just get us to the ferry station."

"Name not Habib. Name Amir."

"Same difference."

As the cab pulled up to the curb, Grandy handed Amir the fare. "Say hi to your brother."

Amir took the money and gave the old redhead a baffled look.

Grandy stood in front of the terminal studying the schedule. "Okay, Rain. Looks like the next one's in ten minutes." She approached the counter.

"Hey Ben." Grandy read the clerk's name tag. "Need one round trip ticket for Alcatraz. I'm assuming you don't charge for babies."

"We only sell round trip tickets," the young man looked at the senior citizen with amusement. And we only charge for the ones who can walk and talk. That'll be thirty-four dollars."

"Thirty-four bucks? For that price I hope you get a meal with the ride." Grandy looked at the sign again. "Wait a minute, there's one for eighteen bucks."

"That's only for the tour around the island. The boat doesn't stop."

"Do you think it could slow down long enough for me to get off? I'm just making a quick delivery."

"No, ma'am. If you want to go onto the island, it will be thirty-four dollars."

"Did you sell a ticket to a young man, about 30, 5' 9", 150 lbs., long, dark hair?"

"Well that describes about half the men who come through here. Sorry."

Grandy looked around the room, but no sign of Dakota.

"Ma'am, if you're not going to buy a ticket, please step aside for the next person in line."

"Don't pop a shirt button. Here." She handed him the cash and Ben gave her a ticket. While Grandy stood in line waiting for the next ferry to Alcatraz, she kept a watchful eye out for Dakota. As soon as the boat was docked and emptied, the new set of passengers filed on. Old Red made her way to the front and sat

41

down next to a young woman dressed in a low-cut, tie-dyed sun dress and pink, hand-crocheted shawl. The lady's headband was adorned with abalone shell beads. Unusual jewelry decorated her fingers, neck and wrists."

"Where did you get those earrings?" Grandy asked.

"Oh, these are actual human bones. I got them at the Bone Room."

"Who do they belong to?"

"The earrings? They're mine."

"No. The bones. Who do the bones belong to? Someone famous?"

A nasal sounding laugh spilled forth from the spike-haired blonde. "I have no idea, didn't even think to ask when I bought them."

"Where did you say you got them?" Grandy asked with great interest.

"The Bone Room. It's over in Berkeley, just across the bridge. Do you like these?" The girl pointed to her collection of dress pins. "They're all real insects, or insect pieces. This is a recluse spider, this is a wing of a stag beetle. Oh, and here, do you like this one? It's part of a scorpion. It's my favorite."

"You got all that stuff at the Bone Room?"

"Sure did."

"Wow. I need to take my friend there." While Grandy knew Bernice would think it was creepy, Charlotte had voiced a fascination with mummies and preserved insects was close enough.

"Where'd you get the tattoo?" The girl pointed to Grandy's chest.

"Los Angeles."

"Cool." She smiled at the senior citizen who was as bizarre in her looks as she was in personality. Her red hair seemed to be a hundred different shades and stood out like a disorganized tornado. She wore a neon green shirt cut just low enough in the front to expose her "Area 51" tattoo. The infant in her arms was wrapped in a blanket with space alien faces sprinkled on it.

"Are you married?" asked Grandy.

The question caught the young lady off guard.

"What?"

"Are you married? You know, hitched, betrothed, going steady? Anything like that?" Grandy looked at her with intensity.

"No. Why do you ask?"

"I know someone you would really like."

"Oh yeah. And who would that be?"

"My son, Dakota."

"Dakota, that's an unusual name. I like it."

"What's your name?"

"Rackna. What's yours?"

"Grandy." Old Red gave her new friend a hearty handshake. "Rackna. What kind of name is that? Is it a planet I haven't heard of?"

"No," replied Rackna, sharing another of her nasal sounding laughs. "It's a nickname I've had since I was a kid. It's short for Arachnoid, because I've always been into spiders."

"You like kids?"

"I love kids. I'm assuming the handsome little baby is your grandson or granddaughter?"

"Yeah, this is Rain, Dakota's kid. You wanna meet Dakota? He's going to be at the prison."

"The prison?"

"No, he's not in prison. I mean, he's meeting us at Alcatraz. They haven't seen each other for a couple of days. I just know he'd love meeting you."

"Sure, why not."

The short ferry ride had come to an end and the sightseers disembarked for their tour. Rackna followed Grandy and Rain.

"Are you taking the tour?"

"Yeah, Dakota's not due to meet me until 2:00 and I paid the darned thirty-four bucks. Might as well."

Looming before the small group were large, grey, cold structures. Wisps of weeds pushed through cracked cement. The ghosts of former angry occupants seemed to hover above the isolated island. As the tourists were ushered in and out of the barracks, the tour guide recited his history lesson. Grandy kept an eye out for Dakota as she had Rackna take photos of her and Rain in one of the cells. When they got to the solitary confinement area, Grandy giggled.

"What's so funny, Grandy?"

"Oh, it's a long story. My friend and I went to a prison back in Wyoming and she almost had a heart attack when she thought I had locked her in solitary."

"You'd like my brother. He's a real jokester, too. He used to play practical jokes on me all the time. He gave up, though, when he realized I wasn't afraid of spiders or other creepy crawlies."

"Where you from?"

"Colorado. I'm just traveling, trying to see as much as I can before I run out of money. I'll be going home soon. I kinda miss the pine trees and mountains. I've seen enough of California."

"I know what you mean."

The tour concluded and Grandy found a place to feed and change Rain. She sent Rackna off to find food for the two adults. When the small group had satisfied their stomachs, they headed back to the ferry dock. It was close to 2:00 and both ladies watched with anticipation the ferry approaching the island. Once it docked, Dakota and his mom spotted each other at the same time. Rain was in his father's arms faster than raw cookie dough disappears from a bowl.

"Ma. What's going on? Why did you pick *this* place to meet? We could have met in the city."

"Couldn't take that chance, Son."

"Nobody's following you, Ma. Avis has to work sometime and Dad wouldn't have enough money to buy penny candy, let alone enough to chase after you."

"Well, Avis has money and he would probably give it to him. Plus your greedy brother hired a PI.. The bald headed jerk might still be after us."

Dakota tried to remain calm as he explained to his mother, "Ma, you can't live like this, paranoid all the time. Just enjoy your life. Don't worry about them." The handsome son hugged his mother then noticed the young woman standing close by.

"Dakota," said Grandy with determination, "there's someone I want you to meet. Rackna, this is Dakota. Dakota, this is my new friend, Rackna. She's on her way back to Colorado. I thought maybe – "

"Ma. I'm not going to Colorado, I'm going to Seattle to meet Skye."

"She needs a ride, Son. Besides, Skye is not a good mother, Rain needs a new one."

"I'm not having this conversation with you again, Ma. No offense, Rackna, but I love Rain's mother very much and whatever my mother said about her is not true." Dakota gave his mother a disapproving stare.

Rackna also gave Grandy a disgusted look but said politely to Dakota, "Don't worry about it and as far as what your mother said, she didn't say a word about you still being happily married. Now, if you'll please excuse me, I need to catch this next ferry back to San Francisco."

"Nice meeting you Rackna," said Dakota.

"Nice meeting you, and Rain too." Rackna didn't say goodbye to Grandy. She just marched down to the ferry and got on.

"Looks like you lost a friend, Ma. You really need to quit trying to fix me up with someone else."

Grandy ignored her son's comment and instead asked him if he was going to tour Alcatraz.

"No, Rain and I are headed back on the next ferry. I want to get to Seattle by Thursday. How about you? Are you staying longer on the island?"

"Just awhile longer. I want to see if I can do some meditation in the Birdman's cell."

Dakota laughed then asked, "Where are you and Bernice headed next?"

"Going to Berkeley tomorrow and then, who knows."

"Ma, I'll call you more often, but you have to promise to answer your cell phone."

"I'll think about it. Remember, you can always listen to the Chet Baxter Show and call in.

"Okay. Well, we need to get going. Take care of yourself, Ma. I love you."

Grandy bent over and gave Rain a kiss on the forehead. "It's been fun, Rain. Bernie will miss your poopy diapers. Bye, you two." Grandy hugged her middle son. "Love you, too." She wiped away a couple of tears as she watched her two favorite boys board the ferry. As soon as they left the dock, Grandy straightened her bony shoulders and walked towards the main building, ready to explore all the places off limit to visitors.

Chapter 13

The sisters, with their fresh hairdos, relaxed at either end of the floral printed sofa. Bernice's fingers kept touching the evenly colored grey hair strands, grateful that after a summer of beauty parlor bombs, she finally had her hair back to her idea of normal. Charlotte's new color and cut however, concerned the younger sister. It seemed as though she was edging towards the "Grandy" look. It was black with frosted white tips and a spike cut that bordered on flyaway.

"Why did you pick such an unflattering style, Char?" Bernice said with a disappointing sigh.

"Just because it's not what you would pick, does not make it unflattering. Besides, I'm starting a new adventure, why not a new look?"

"Well, I think-"

"Let's not talk about my hair, Bernice, let's have something to eat."

Too exhausted to make the trek to the dining hall for dinner, the two opted for a can of soup and crackers.

* * * * *

After their meal, Bernice and Charlotte relaxed once again on the couch. Boxes filled the room, along with two large suitcases.

Bernice glanced at the clock on the wall. "It's getting late, I sure hope Grandy didn't get lost."

"Somehow Grandy doesn't seem the type to get lost. And if she did, she certainly wouldn't tell us about it once she finds her way."

"You're right about that," said Bernice.

"I'm sure she'll be along soon."

"But what if she forgot the name of this place? Or what if there was an accident?"

"Bernice. Stop. You're getting yourself worked up for nothing. You gotta have a little faith."

Bernice had nearly talked herself into a panic attack, when Grandy burst through the door. She picked up Ditch and grunted a hello to the gals.

"How was the trip to Alcatraz, Grandy?" asked Charlotte.

"Except for passing Rain back to Dakota, it was better than a weekend doing taxidermy!" Grandy opened Charlotte's refrigerator door and took a gulp of orange juice from the carton.

"Grandy! That is so rude!" Bernice exclaimed.

"Chill Bernie, Charlie doesn't care. Here." The feisty redhead threw a brown paper bag onto the kitchen table. "I brought you a surprise."

"What is it?" asked a cautious Bernice as she peeked inside.

"I had myself a crab, thought you might want the shells, make yourself a necklace or something."

"But they're all broken. Yuck! It smells." Scrunching her nose, Bernice closed the bag tightly and threw it back on the table.

"I had to crack it to get the meat out. Boy was it good."

There was a sliver of hesitation in Charlotte's decision to go on the road with Grandy. Her sister had warned her of her roommate's "minor" idiosyncrasies. While she thought them anything but minor, she was certain the trip would provide more excitement than she would ever experience at Bayside.

Grandy surveyed the room. "Where do you think we're gonna put all those boxes? I thought you said you were only traveling with us for a little while?"

"I'm only taking those two suitcases and that small box." Charlotte pointed towards the front door. Salvation Army will be by tomorrow to pick up the rest. My sister, the organizer, convinced me it was all junk. I've always been somewhat of a pack rat."

"Got any good stuff?" asked Grandy, peeking inside one of the large boxes.

"Depends on what you consider good."

"Get out of that box, Grandy, we don't need any more rubbish in the motor home," Bernice said tartly. She squeezed her eyes shut, remembering their stop at the storage unit in Minnesota before their trip.

"You calling your sister's stuff and my stuff rubbish? That's not very nice, Bernie. I don't complain about your four hundred jars of nail polish or your boxes of Depends that take up most of the closet space in the motor home." Grandy gave her traveling companion a look that dared her to challenge back.

"If you -"

Charlotte interrupted the showdown,"Okay, Ladies, how about a nightcap before we retire for the evening?"

"Make mine a double and add three black olives," said Grandy as she rummaged around in the boxes. She salvaged several items of interest, including a miniature pyramid made of varnished sugar cubes, a 1989 *Ripley's Believe or Not* calendar, a wind chime constructed of used toothbrushes and a baseball cap with brightly colored feathers glued to it.

"Bernie was going to make you get rid of these gems? I've got the perfect use for every one of them."

Trying to maintain a dignified composure and not sound like she was belly aching, Bernice said, "Are you sure you really need those items? Won't the motor home get a bit crowded?"

Grandy shot her friend a look that clearly meant "be quiet."

"So where are we headed tomorrow, Grandy?" asked Charlotte, quickly trying to change the subject.

"Seattle."

"Seattle? I thought we could spend more time along the coastline," Bernice said, clearly disappointed.

"Rain's mother is in Seattle. I have to see what kinda mother would leave her kid and then I'm gonna give her a piece of my mind. And speaking of mind, did you call Chet?"

"Yes, I handled it."

"What'd you tell him?"

"I told him you went to the San Francisco Zoo."

"Did you have to be so specific about which zoo? If Avis is listening to that program, he'll be hot on our tail again."

"Well, you told me to use my imagination and that's what slipped out when I was imagining."

"Honestly Bernie, you're going to land us in big trouble."

Charlotte decided it was time to once again step in as peacekeeper. "Now, Girls, it's only a 13 or 14 hour drive. Today's only Monday. If we leave early tomorrow, we can do this, with time to spare."

Grandy grabbed Ditch and opened the door. "Come on Bernice, let's go to the motor home."

"I'm spending the night at Charlotte's."

"Fine. But be ready at 5 a.m. We'll eat on the road." Grandy stormed out the door.

The sisters gave each other a look of resolve and readied themselves for bed.

Chapter 14

"Charlotte... Charlotte..." Bernice shook her sleeping sister.
"What... What's wrong?"

"Somebody's outside the window." Extensive fear ruled Bernice's voice and her begonia pink fingernails dug into her sister's arm.

"Ouch!" Charlotte instantly sat up and brought herself into full consciousness. She rubbed her eyes and reached for her glasses. "What time is it?"

"Somebody's trying to break in!" By now the younger sister's demeanor had escalated into an expansive panic. "Call the police. Do you have a weapon handy?"

Another sharp rap on the window caused Charlotte to jump out of bed and walk to the window.

"What are you doing, Charlotte?!" screeched Bernice, "you're going to get us killed!"

Charlotte looked out the window and saw Grandy's prune shaped face staring back at her. "It's just Grandy," she said with air of irritation.

Bernice joined her sister at the window and shouted, "What are you doing, Grandy?"

"The front door was locked. You've got five minutes to get your fannies out here, or I'm leavin' without ya."

"Keep it down over there!" Charlotte's next door neighbor banged on the adjoining wall.

"We're comin', just wait a few minutes," Bernice pleaded with Grandy.

"Five, that's all." Grandy returned to the motor home.

"She's kidding, right? Five minutes?" asked a shocked Charlotte.

"Grandy never kids about anything. Just grab your stuff and we can get dressed on the road."

The sisters gathered their things and slipped down the hall. Charlotte's mind quickly processed the last couple of days and realized it was going to take a tremendous amount of patience to travel with Old Red.

"Where ya goin', Char?" asked Norma, a round, nearly bald-headed resident, as she peeked out of her door.

"I'm going on a little trip with my sister and her friend."

"Where you going to?"

"Not sure yet, Norma. I guess wherever Grandy wants to."

"Grandy? Now where have I heard that name before?"

"Grandy and my sister Bernice are the traveling grandmas on the Chet Baxter show," Charlotte said with pride.

"Land sakes!" Norma pointed at the smug faced Bernice. "I listen to you every day on the radio. I heard you were in San Francisco. Can I have your autograph? Do you think Grandy could give me one, too?" Norma looked up and down the hall for the other half of the traveling duo.

"Well, she's kinda irritable this morning, but you can have mine. You got a pen?" Bernice stretched her chest out a bit and prepared herself for the autograph.

"Just a sec." Norma went inside and quickly returned with a tube of lipstick and prescription receipt. "I'm sorry, that's all I can find on such short notice. Can you write, 'To Norma, You are one cool chick. Love, Bernice.'" As Bernice scribbled, Norma fired several questions at Charlotte. "Are you going to be on the radio, too? When ya comin' back? Make sure you send us postcards, we'll miss you at yoga."

"I'm not sure, Norma.. That reminds me though, I have to go back and grab my yoga DVD."

Grandy leaned on the horn and woke a few more residents.

"Let's go, Charlotte!" Bernice uttered in a loud whisper. Charlotte took one last quick survey of her apartment, locked her door and joined her sibling.

Norma waved the paper with Bernice's autograph and pointed to the front door as the sisters hobbled to the motor home. "Have fun Ladies, don't forget about us!"

By the time the two sisters were entering the Fleetwood, a group of elderly residents had congregated at the front door, most of them trying to figure out what all the commotion was about. As Grandy exited the parking lot at high speed, she laid on the horn.

Trying to get dressed and apply makeup was almost impossible for Bernice and Charlotte as Grandy maneuvered the streets of San Francisco for one last time.

"How long has Grandy been driving this vehicle?" asked Charlotte with a hint of uncertainty in her voice.

"Not long enough," an exasperated Bernice responded.

* * * * *

Bernice planted her ample bottom into the motor home passenger seat as she waited for Charlotte to finish getting ready. She smiled to herself as the rising sun turned the lead gray morning into a promise of opportunity. The only spoilage was the steel lines of vehicles stretching for miles. She reached for the radio knobs to find a peaceful station to listen to.

"What are you doing?"

"Looking for a Christian radio station, Grandy. I need something calming to listen to this time of morning."

When there was no argument or sarcastic comment, Bernice nonchalantly looked at her best friend. "Was Grandy feeling okay?" she wondered to herself.

Charlotte made her way to the front of the motor home and asked the girls in a peppy voice, "When's breakfast? I'm starved!"

"Do you like Burger King or McDonald's?" Grandy asked.

"Oh, I don't know. Why don't we really treat ourselves and indulge at a Denny's."

Grandy thought a moment, "That's fine, Charlie. It's going to be awhile before the surprise I have for you is ready anyway."

"Surprise? What kind of surprise?" Charlotte asked, curiosity taking a seat in her mind.

A jilted and pouting Bernice inquired, "Do I get a surprise too, Grandy?"

"If you want to, but I doubt you'll like it."

"How do you know? Maybe I will find it interesting. Why don't you tell us what it is so we can get ready for it."

Grandy glanced at the two sisters, their faces nearly blocking her view of the road. The look of immense anticipation filled the air like a giant banner. "You won't need to get ready, just have money so you can participate."

Charlotte looked at her sibling with a huge grin. Bernice said flatly, "Don't get too excited, Char, we'll probably end up somewhere weird, like the hall of fame for ceramic elephants or the world's largest dog biscuit."

Grandy's clipped response to her friend's comment was typical, "Shows how much you know, Bernie, neither one of those places are on the West Coast, you have to go much farther east to see those treasures."

Chapter 15

"Avis Wayland."

"Hey, Avis. It's your old man. How's it goin'?"

"I'm on my way to court, Dad. Make it quick." Avis rolled his tired green eyes as he stuffed legal papers into his briefcase.

"Any word on your mother?"

"No, but I'm working on it. I really need to get going, Dad. I have a settlement hearing in fifteen minutes."

"Wait, I need you to wire me some cash."

"What?"

"Yeah, I'm stuck here in South Dakota with a busted fuel pump."

"What are you doing in South Dakota?"

"I told you I was in kind of a bind. I need to crash at your place for a few days."

"And I told you that was not such a good idea. Call Howard."

"I already did. He said no. Said he didn't have any room because his wife's brother was staying with them."

"That's too bad, but you can't stay with us. I'll wire you some money later today."

"Come on, Son. Have a heart. After all we've been through together. Besides, tell your pretty little lady, Lucy, that she won't even know I'm there."

"Because you WON'T be there. And her name is Liza." Avis paced impatiently and looked at the clock.

"You're not gonna deprive me of getting to know my little granddaughter, Georgia?"

"Her name is Augusta, Dad, and I really need to go. Stay on the line and I'll have my secretary get the details where you're staying so I can get you the money. Bye, Dad."

Avis hung up the phone before Lester could try another argument. He then gave quick instructions to his secretary as he hurried out the door.

* * * * *

While the mechanic worked on Lester's battered pickup, he kept up a ping-pong conversation in his head concerning the reasons his own sons didn't want him around. Mostly he was convinced it was because their mother had told them all kinds of lies about him. "She never was supportive of me," he muttered to himself. "A couple of meaningless flings through the years and the old woman wants to put my private parts into a blender." Still convinced he was entitled to half of the motor home she was driving, Lester decided to try a new approach to his immediate situation, which began with a second phone call to the home of his youngest son, Howard.

* * * * *

"Hello."

"Blackie? Is that you?"

"Yeah. Who's this?"

"This is your father-in-law."

"Oh. Howard's not here."

"I know, I'm calling to talk to you."

"What about?" A nervous wave splashed into the woman's throat.

"Howard said you didn't have room for me to stay with you for a couple nights because of your brother visiting," Lester tried what he hoped was a sympathetic voice pitch as he continued, "but I'm *really* desperate here, Blackie. I need a place to lay my head, just for a couple of nights."

There was a long capsule of silence before Blackie said, "Mr. Wayland, I'll talk to Howard and let you know. Where can I call you back at?"

Pure frustration now embalmed Lester, "Damn it, Blackie! Never mind about asking Howard, just tell him I'm on my way and I'll be at your house in a couple of days!" A dial tone followed his proclamation.

* * * * *

"Hello?"

"Hey, Babe, it's me." Blackie's voice exuded panic.

"What's wrong, Honey?"

"Your disgusting father just called. He said to tell you he's on his way here."

"What do you mean? I just talked to him and told him he couldn't stay with us."

"He said he's coming to visit and he sounded real mad."

"Don't worry, I'll handle it."

"Can your dad stay with Avis?"

"He's going to Hawaii. Not sure when he's coming back but maybe Dad can stay with him after he returns."

"What if he won't let him stay there either?" Howard could clearly visualize Blackie nervously rubbing her "genie and a lamp" ankle tattoo in hopes it would grant her a wish.

"Blackie, I promise, it will all work out. You've got me, your brother and my poker game buddies to take care of the situation. Go relax and watch your soaps. I'll be home in a few short hours."

"Okay. I love you."

"I love you, too. Bye."

Howard blew out a large breath and tried to concentrate on his driving. Memories of his childhood kept leaping in front of him though; a mother, caring, kind but a curator of bizarre ideas and a father so engrossed in his own fleshly desires that it was a wonder he didn't end up owning an escort service. Howard decided to focus on the task at hand. He was grateful his next beer delivery was only a quarter mile up the road.

Chapter 16

The Fleetwood was corralled by an endless sea of vehicles, the result of the daily Bay Area commute. Heat waves echoed off the rooftops like a desert mirage. It was evident to Grandy that the migrating modes of transportation were equivalent to what she and Bernice had encountered during their trip to Los Angeles. It didn't take long before impatience dominated Grandy. She rolled down the window, stuck her head out and stretched her neck as far as possible, trying to see past the idling semi-truck in front of her. Heavy, black smoke from the truck's stack rolled into her face. A cough shook the redhead's body, she cursed then quickly rolled up the window.

"What's wrong, Old Lady," said Bernice with an air of amusement. To her, Grandy's swearing always sounded like it was a language she was just learning to use.

"How hard is it to keep driving down the road? What keeps stopping all these idiots, anyway?" mumbled Grandy.

"There's probably an accident on the bridge," Charlotte interjected. "We're going be here for a while. Happens all the time."

"I told you we should have left at 5," Grandy growled.

"You didn't wake up either," Bernice said defensively.

"You need to call Chet, Bernie."

"It's too early, the show hasn't started yet."

"I don't care, wake him up. We won't have time later."

"I'll call later, when the show is actually on."

Grandy ignored her friend's reply, proceeded to put the motor home in park, unbuckled her seatbelt and headed for the door.

"Where are you going?" asked Bernice.

"To see what's going on." Grandy said as she exited the motor home.

"I don't think you should be doing that!" Bernice yelled. "We could get a ticket, or get towed, or somebody could -"

"Hey, Bernice, how about some yoga? You do have a DVD player, don't you?"

The bizarre question from Charlotte stopped Bernice in mid-sentence. She gawked at her sister as complete defeat dressed her body.

"You want to exercise now? We're stuck in the middle of the freeway without a driver and you're worried about your waistline?"

"Deep breathing exercises, Bernice, that's what it's all about."

Bernice started to experience the helplessness she felt every time Grandy put her in an uncomfortable situation. Only this time it was her own flesh and blood that had joined the team of "Dumb and Dumber." At a loss for words, Bernice responded, "The DVD player is in the cupboard by the T.V."

"Would you like to join me?"

"No thank you, I'll pass. I might pull a muscle or something."

"Nonsense. If anything, it'll make you feel ten years younger."

"That's okay, I'll just keep a look out for Grandy."

Charlotte set up the DVD player and positioned herself on her yoga mat. Bernice watched as her sister maneuvered her body into poses she never imagined possible. Even Ditch seemed unconcerned about Grandy as he lay down beside Charlotte and stretched out his small shaggy body.

Bernice went and sat in the passenger seat, her head in a constant swivel trying to track down her off-balanced traveling companion.

"How long do you think we'll have to sit here, Charlotte?"

"Oh," Charlotte answered in between her long breathing exercise, "it could be a couple of minutes or a couple of hours. Depends on how bad it is."

* * * * *

Grandy worked her way around the mass of cars and trucks. Drivers either honked, waved, smiled or gave her the one finger salute. For each gesture she responded in like fashion. As she wandered between lines of vehicles, bumper sticker slogans caught her eye. "Ralph Nader for President," "Hummer Hater," "Poets for Peace." As she passed a car donning a "Treehugger on Board" bumper sticker, she stared intently at the driver. The middle-aged woman with long, gray, braided hair shouted through her window, "What are you looking at?"

"Just wanted to see what a treehugger looked like." Grandy answered as she continued through the traffic jam. She soon reached the scene of the accident. Approaching an officer who was directing traffic, she asked, "How much longer you gonna be? My friends and I need to get going."

The young, acne-scarred rookie stared at the senior citizen before him. Her multi-shaded red hair was hung like deflating ringlets around her well wrinkled face. There was no mistaking the piercing blue eyes demanding an answer from him. Even more disturbing though, was the tee shirt she was wearing; Metallic black in color, a large silver flying saucer across the chest with the words, "There's No Place Like Home" imprinted on it. Honking horns quickly brought the highway patrolman back to reality.

"Ma'am, you need to get back in your vehicle. It's too dangerous to be out here."

"I just need to know when this mess will be cleaned up."

"Soon. Now get back to your vehicle before I have you arrested."

"On what charge?" Grandy's voice contained a tone of strong indignation.

"Threatening an officer."

"How do you figure that?"

"Your appearance."

* * * * *

"I sure hope Grandy gets back soon." Bernice's nerves had her opening the refrigerator door in search of nothing in particular. She filled Ditch's water dish, then wandered back to the front of the motor home to watch for Grandy. After five very long minutes, Bernice spotted her wayward friend.

"There she is!" As Bernice opened the door for her approaching friend, Ditch let loose a large bark and ran out the door.

"Ditch!" Bernice screamed. "Come back here!" She began to cry hysterically. "If he gets hit by a car Grandy will kill me! Ditch!"

"Relax Bernice, we'll get him or maybe he'll run straight to Grandy." Charlotte unfolded herself from her latest yoga position and walked over to her sibling.

"Come on, we'll both go get him," she grabbed the frantic woman's arm and pulled her out the door.

"We can't both leave the motor home. Somebody needs to stay and watch it so a car jacker doesn't try to steal it."

Charlotte gave Bernice a bemused look. "Where's he going to go? The traffic is at a stand still."

"I still think -"

"Let's go, Bernice, the motor home will be fine."

The two properly coiffed woman began walking between the lanes of traffic calling for Ditch. This time drivers sitting in their vehicles dared to roll down their windows enough to ask what was going on.

"I'm trying to find Ditch," answered Bernice.

"Ditch?" asked bewildered commuters.

"Yeah, he's my roommate's dog." And with no further explanation, she continued to do a fast waddle with her cane down the middle of the road.

It was only a minute later when the three ladies and the dog managed to meet up next to a fifty-something, long-haired dude on a chopper.

"What are you and Ditch doing out here?" Grandy asked with irritation as she picked up her dog.

"I saw you coming, opened the door and the little mutt ran out. Charlotte and I were trying to catch him." The pitch of Bernice's voice kept rising the more she talked.

"You let -"

"It was an accident, Grandy, really," By now Bernice was breathing heavily and a layer of sweat from her forehead was sliding south. Her grey eyes were wide with fear.

"Ditch seems to be just fine, get back to the motor home before you get run over." Grandy patted her friend's back then gave her a slight shove towards their vehicle.

Bernice and Charlotte headed towards the motor home thinking Grandy was right behind them. A glance over their shoulders showed them that their eccentric friend was engrossed in a conversation with the guy on the chopper.

"What do you think they're talking about, Bernice?" asked Char.

"Knowing Grandy, she's probably trying to make a trade. Me for the motorcycle."

Chapter 17

There wasn't much space available in the Berkeley Denny's parking lot. That meant nothing to Grandy though; she simply pulled in behind other vehicles and turned off the engine.

"You can't park here," a mortified Bernice said. "People will be screaming at us that we are blocking their cars."

"They'll get over it," Old Red responded and marched towards the restaurant.

Realizing there was little they could do about the parking situation, the two sisters followed their crazy friend into Denny's.

Almost immediately after being seated at a booth, the waitress appeared – a fifty something, 5'6' woman, built like a square box. "Peach" was stamped on her name tag. Peach's fingernails were long and painted the same color as her hair, a nearly marigold yellow. Even her Botox lips were outlined in a pale version of a yellow mustard color.

"Would you like coffee?" she asked in a voice meant to sound like sunshine.

Grandy's long thick knuckled finger pointed first to the coffee mug on her left, then to the one on her right. "Fill them both up."

Peach hesitated only a moment before obeying Grandy's wish.

"I'll take orange/honey tea, please," said Bernice.

"And I'll have herbal tea," Charlotte added.

"I'll be right back with your tea and to take your order."

"That woman needs to tone down the color yellow, I'm goin' to need sunglasses if I have to look at her too many times," Grandy said as she poured three packets of sugar into one the coffee cups.

Surprise was evident on Bernice's face and she asked, "Since when did you start putting sugar in your coffee? You've always drank it black."

"Not always. You didn't know me when I was younger, you have no idea what I used to put in my coffee." Grandy looked irritated at her friend's assumption.

Peach returned with the tea and asked for the ladies' orders.

Grandy ordered the hungry man breakfast of biscuits and gravy, eggs, bacon and toast.

"I'll have an English muffin and a small order of fresh fruit." Bernice removed her baggie of pills from her purse.

"I'll have a bowl of oatmeal with strawberries and wheat toast." Charlotte pulled out her Sunday through Saturday pill dispenser.

"I don't know why you two old farts worry so much about your figures. If Prince Charming showed up, he'd be young enough to be your grandson."

"It's about good health, Grandy, not men," said Charlotte. "All that cholesterol is gonna clog up your arteries."

"My arteries are fine. Your arteries are gonna get plugged up with all them pills."

"These are only vitamins, Grandy. I'll never take any of those prescription meds again. That's what got me so messed up in the head."

"You better tell your sister, I think they're messing with her head."

Bernice said defensively, "I *have* to take these pills, doctor's orders."

Charlotte touched her sister's hand gently, "What do you think would happen if you stopped taking them? I stopped and look at me. Just something to think about, Dear."

66

The conversation took a sudden turn when Grandy announced, "I think I'm gonna call Dog Face today."

"Oh, no, what for?" asked Bernice as previous nightmares of Grandy's brother resurfaced.

"I want my scooters.

"We don't need the scooters. Besides, there is only two scooters and three of us."

"Who's Dog Face?" asked Charlotte.

"Grandy's brother, and somebody you don't want to meet, said Bernice nervously."

"Hey," Grandy's voice had become stern, "my brother helped us out a lot while we were getting ready to leave Minnesota, especially with Nick. As for the scooters, I was thinking of me and Charlie going for a ride, not you."

"Who is Nick?" A tone of inquisitiveness filled Char's voice.

"I'll tell you later," Bernice said as sweat beneath her armpits formed at the thought of Dog Face, scooters and the near death incident with Nick.

"Wait a minute!" It was Charlotte's turn to demand attention. "Tell me now about Dog Face and Nick. What happened that it upsets Bernice so much?"

"Nothing," Grandy said.

"I'll tell you," Bernice said as she took a quick gulp of tea. "Grandy's brother, Dog Face is smelly, rude and obnoxious. He always wants to kiss my hand but ends up slobbering nasty tobacco on it. And then he tried to help us with Nick who, was, is, a resident at the retirement home we were at. We thought he died in the motor home and Dog Face helped us put him back in the retirement home in the hopes the staff would think he died while watching TV but, as we were leaving to go on our trip, he came back to life and said good bye to me." Bernice closed her eyelids and sat back against the chair. She was clearly exhausted from the memories she had just shared.

Charlotte watched her sister for a moment then looked over at Grandy with a stunned expression. "Well, it sounds like you both had quit an adventure before you even got started on your trip," Charlotte was talking slowly and carefully.

"You don't know the half of it," Bernice said.

A large smile then spread over the older sister's face and she said in an excited voice, "Sounds like fun! Hope *we* have times like that."

Bernice opened her worried eyes and looked at her sister with caution. "Oh no," she thought to herself, "My sister is turning into another Grandy."

Before anything more could be said, Peach served them their food, then asked, "Is that your Fleetwood motor home in the parking lot blocking cars?"

"Yeah," said Grandy.

"You need to move it, that couple over there needs to leave."

"They can wait until I'm done eating," Grandy replied.

"Sorry, you really need to move your vehicle," Peach said firmly.

"Okay, but don't serve our food until I get back, I don't want it cold."

Peach went back to the kitchen with the platters until Grandy returned from moving the coach.

"Okay, we're ready!" Grandy shouted to the waitress as she sat back down.

Bernice and Charlotte hadn't said much while Old Red was gone. The thought of telling Grandy, "I told you so" had crossed Bernice's mind but she decided against it. Probably wouldn't be good for her health.

After nearly inhaling her hardy meal, Grandy wrapped two pieces of bacon in a napkin. "I'm gonna go feed Ditch. Thanks for the grub, Charlie. You two hurry along, it's almost time to call Chet."

Bernice and Charlotte sipped on their tea while waiting for the tab. "She certainly keeps life on the edge," Charlotte noted.

"Never a dull moment. I hope she forgets about the scooters."

"Why? They sound like fun. Besides, she said her and I would be riding them."

"Yeah, well, I still expect she'll find some way to embarrass me with them."

"Oh, Bernice, lighten up."

"What do you mean? Grandy's the one who needs to lighten up."

"Grandy's funny. I like her."

"I do too, Charlotte, but sometimes her choices are a bit -"

"Unorthodox?"

"No, weird, just plain weird."

Chapter 18

As Charlotte and Bernice entered the motor home, Grandy was on the phone with Chet. "Here they are now," she announced. "Chet wants to talk to you, Charlie."

A bewildered look spread over Charlotte's face and she asked in a whisper, "What am I supposed to say?"

"Anything you want as long as you don't tell him exactly where we are."

Charlotte smiled and spoke into the phone which was on speaker mode, "Hi Chet, this is Char."

"How you doin' Char? Are you enjoying traveling with Grandy and your sister?"

Chet's voice was soothing, like rich hot chocolate on a cold night. Charlotte was visualizing the radio host Bernice had described to her; a middle-aged man with thick, dark hair and captivating blue eyes.

"So far so good, it's only been a few hours. We haven't seen much yet, but we've already encountered two incidents."

"What kind of incidents?" Chet asked with a slight concern in his voice. Experience had taught him to screen the information coming in from Grandy and Bernice. And since he didn't know Char, he was trying to ire on the side of caution with her, too.

"Well, -" Charlotte hesitated, she looked at Grandy.

"What?" the redhead asked. "Tell him, that's why we call in, to tell people about our trip."

Chet grinned to himself as he listened to the two old ladies yapping away and wondered when Bernice would wiggle her way into the conversation.

The newest member of the traveling trio started speaking again, "We were stuck on the Bay Bridge out of San Francisco this morning for two hours because of an accident."

"You were in an accident?"

"Oh, no Chet. We were just stuck behind an accident."

"What was the other incident?"

"It concerned Grandy's dog."

"Yeah, they let Ditch out on the freeway and he almost got killed!" Grandy shouted.

"Is he okay?"

Grandy continued, "He's a little shook up. I just gave him some bacon."

"So where are you headed?"

"You know we can't tell you that, Chet. Why do you keep asking us? My no good ex and greedy son may be still following us."

"Sorry Grandy, I forgot."

"I see the phones are lit up. Are you ladies ready to take a couple of calls?"

"Depends on who is it," Grandy said.

"Let's take this one from San Francisco. Leon, you're on the line, what's your question?"

"My question is for Bernice."

Bernice put her face close to the phone, cleared her voice and straightened her blouse. "Yes Leon?" she said in a gag me sweet tone of voice.

"If you're gonna be in the Bay Area long, I'd like you to accompany me to the symphony sometime."

"Sorry, Leon, we're not in San Francisco any longer. We're - "

Charlotte interrupted, "I'll be coming back to San Francisco someday. I'll go with you to the symphony."

Leon's voice hesitated as he tried to figure out what to say to Charlotte. "Sure, I'll give you a jingle." Then Leon hung up.

"Okay, onto the next caller," said Chet. "We have Penny in Tempe, Arizona."

"Hey Grandy, and Bernice. Just wanted to tell you how much I enjoy hearing your stories. My husband and I retired and moved down here to Tempe a few years ago. It's so hot in the summer, we thought we'd leave for a couple of months. My husband wants to drive the car and just stay in hotels. I heard you guys on the radio and thought we should get a motor home and do like you."

"You don't have any ungrateful children that will chase after you, do you?" Grandy asked.

"Uh, no," Penny said, a bit surprised by the question.

"Well, if you need directions or instructions concerning the Star Trek Fest, ask Chet, he can tell you all about it."

"Okay.

"Penny," Bernice was now determined to give her opinion. "If your husband really wants to drive a car and stay in hotels, I would consider his suggestion. Especially if the places have a Jacuzzi and a nice restaurant."

"But a motor home sounds like so much more fun. Isn't it Grandy?" Penny was clearly looking for support.

"Of course it's more fun. You have everything you need; a kitchen, bed and toilet right at your fingertips. Not to mention you have more room for a dog and any other strays you might pick up." Grandy glanced over at Char and gave her a wink.

"Well, thank you, Grandy and Bernice. That's what we love about you two, you're like the *Odd Couple,* like *Tom and Jerry,* or..."

"Or like French wine and moonshine?" Charlotte said.

"You got that one right, Char. Hey, we're about out of time for today, Ladies. You'll call us back tomorrow, right?" asked Chet.

"If the creek don't rise above my bloomers," answered Grandy.

Chapter 19

"Are you ready for your surprise, Charlie?"

"What is it? What is it?" asked Bernice, not wanting to be excluded from anything.

Grandy gave her friend a chafing glance and said, "I was talking to your sister."

"What about me?" Bernice's lip began to form a quivering pout. "How do you know I won't like it?"

"Because I know you, and I know you won't like it."

Bernice started to protest but Charlotte intervened, "Let's go and check out the surprise together. I bet we'll all have a good time."

"Fine," said Grandy, "but if Bernie makes one more comment, she's sitting in the camper with Ditch."

* * * * *

The three traveling companions walked towards Grandy's secret plan. Being unusual characters themselves, they blended perfectly with the Berkeley landscape. A teenage boy with a purple Mohawk and several piercings walked past them. A banner was draped around his shoulders with the words "Love Not War" painted on it. The protestor stared at the elderly ladies as though *they* were the ones out of place in this city.

"That's just shameful," Bernice said stiffly.

"What is? Protesting?" asked Charlotte.

"No, that hair and all those earrings on his face are not natural. They look terrible."

Grandy joined the conversation, "It's called 'expressing your individualism,' Bernie. He probably stared at you because of your hair and outfit."

"What's wrong with my hair and outfit?"

"Your hair is the same shade of blue as the veins in your neck and you shouldn't wear white capris, the lower half of your body looks like turkey drum sticks wrapped in toilet paper."

"Yeah, well, just so you know Grandy, your appearance is so twisted that NASA wouldn't even take you for observation," Bernice retorted.

Before an argument could escalate, the travelers passed an older gentleman with long, greasy, hair playing a guitar, his large brown eyes gave Bernice a soulful look. His guitar case lay open beside him, waiting for money to fill its torn red velvet lining.

Bernice started to reach in her purse for some change when Char put her hand on top of her sister's. "Don't Bernice, most of these street people make more money in a day than you or I could make in a week."

"But look at him, he looks homeless and sad."

"Of course he looks that way. He chooses to. Bet he probably lives in a high rise in downtown San Francisco."

Grandy turned around and walked back to the guitar man. Bernice and Charlotte couldn't hear what they were talking about but when she returned, she was smiling.

"What did he say?" The two sisters said in unison.

"Nothing you would care about, but just so you don't keep bugging me, I'll tell you. Acer said there's a reunion in South Carolina of the surviving members from the 1947 Roswell incident."

Bernice shook her head. Charlotte chose to ask questions. "That's a different name, Acer."

"Yeah, he's named after a minor planet."

"When you said the surviving members of Roswell, I'm assuming you mean the military personnel that investigated the incident."

"Who else Charlie? You don't think the aliens themselves would make a public announcement of their reunion, do you?"

"Of course not, Grandy. How silly of me."

* * * * *

Five minutes later the trio was standing in front of a white building with a large black awning.

"The Bone Room?" disillusionment echoed in Bernice's voice. "What kind of place is this? Do I need to worry about being part of an experiment?"

"Relax my friend, this is a place of unique natural history and fun stuff to buy," Grandy said.

"Come on, Sister," said Charlotte, "we at least need to give it a chance."

Bernice groaned and reluctantly following the other two into the store. Grandy promptly left the group and wandered off to explore by herself. Charlotte picked up a couple of brochures and began to read them to Bernice.

"It says The Bone Room was created in 1987 by a man named Ron Cauble who uses it as an excuse to learn about natural history. This place is filled with every kind of insect you can think of including many exotic ones. There are bones and skulls of every kind of animal imaginable. The best part is we can buy them, even the human skulls!" Bernice was a bit unnerved by her sister's enthusiasm.

A wave of nausea descended on the younger sister's stomach. She grabbed one of the brochures and began fanning herself.

"You okay, Bernice?" asked Charlotte.

"I'm fine. You go ahead and enjoy the place. I'm just going to sit down for a minute."

"Are you sure? Can I get you anything?"

"No, please go ahead Charlotte, I'll be fine."

"Okay, I'll be back in a little while to check on you."

* * * * *

A college-aged clerk with a black bug earring in his lip walked over to Bernice and asked if she needed help.

"No, thank you." Bernice was quiet a moment before she continued, "I didn't realize it was legal to sell human bones."

"Oh yeah, it's absolutely legal. I'd be happy to show you our best sellers."

"Thanks anyway. If you don't mind, I'm just going to sit here and wait for my sister and my friend."

"Not a problem."

* * * * *

Grandy meanwhile, had walked briskly by the insects and fossils. She was on a mission to find an alien skull. Charlotte found all aspects of The Bone Room delightful and asked a middle-aged saleswoman dressed in a long, multi-colored skirt, T-shirt and army boots many questions. After an hour, Charlotte went back to check on her sister and inquired if she wanted to go and look at the jewelry in the store.

"I don't think I'll find anything there I'll like. You go ahead Char, I'll wait for you here." And she began fanning herself again.

* * * * *

"Look at these earrings, Grandy," Charlotte held a cockroach up to her ear.

"I like the rattlesnake fang earrings, but I'm not here to buy jewelry. I'm going to buy a skull."

"Are you getting a mammal or human one?" Charlotte asked.

"Not sure yet. Maybe one of each." Grandy began to examine more closely the skull prices. She decided she could get an Egyptian Fruit Bat skull and a Cabybera skull for just over $350 or one human skull for $400. It was a hard decision, but Grandy figured she could always find mammal skulls along the side the road so she sprung for the human skull.

* * * * *

The shoppers returned to their motor home to find a homeless man standing on a step stool washing the windshield. Grandy watched him for a minute or so and then remarked, "You missed a spot."

The man gave her an angry look then promptly quit what he was doing and grabbed his stuff to go.

"Just a minute," said Charlotte. She took out a five dollar bill and handed it to him. "Thank you and don't mind the redhead, she's always a bit ill tempered."

"Thank you, Ma'am," and he limped away.

"Why did you give *him* money? You just told me a little while ago not to give that sidewalk guitar player anything," Bernice scolded.

"This guy is most likely a Veteran, somebody who sacrificed for our freedom." Charlotte preached with passionate authority.

"And how do you know the guitar player wasn't?" Charlotte was quite indignant.

"Trust me, Sister, I know the difference."

* * * * *

Inside the motor home, Grandy and Charlotte compared their purchases.

Grandy held up her human skull and proudly announced, "I'm going to name him Berk."

"That is just disgusting, Grandy," Bernice wrinkled her nose and shuttered. "You're not showing any respect for the deceased."

"Hey, I'm naming him, ain't I? Berk is short for Berkeley. Besides, he'll receive more attention from me than sitting on a shelf in that store."

Charlotte pulled her purchases from the bag and laid the cockroach earrings on the table. "These are the store's most popular jewelry item."

"I don't know what the excitement is all about, it's just dead insects," Bernice said wryly, "you can get the same thing from the camper windshield."

"Or at the Road Kill Café," Charlotte said as she tried to bring a smile to Bernice's face. "Here you are, Sister, I got you something." Charlotte handed her a small box.

Bernice did not say what she was thinking, hoping she was wrong and that it was not a matching pair of cockroach earrings like her sister's. She cautiously opened the package. To her surprise it was a small, framed butterfly with colorful yellow, red and green wings. "It's beautiful!" Bernice exclaimed. "I didn't see anything like this in there. Thank you, Char."

"You're welcome." As the siblings gave each other a hug, Grandy's gravelly voice interrupted the sentimental moment, "Alright, buckle up, Gals, we're on our way north to find Bigfoot."

Chapter 20

Grandy played on Bernice's sympathy to get her to relinquish the front passenger seat to her sister. "Poor Charlie, she's hasn't been out and about for awhile, you know what it was like."

"Fine. I'll go lie down, I'm a little tired anyway." Bernice was certain Grandy just wanted to talk about her behind her back so she kept the door to the bedroom open a crack. Normally Ditch would try to lay on the bed with her, but instead he curled up on Charlotte's lap.

"It was sure nice of you to let me come along, Grandy. I'm having a great time." Charlotte scratched Ditch's neck. "How did you know about The Bone Room? I've lived here all my life and never heard about it."

"From a girl I met yesterday at Alcatraz."

"Well, thank you again, I thoroughly enjoyed the place."

After a moment of silence, Grandy started the conversation in a different direction. "You sure aren't anything like your sister. Are you sure she wasn't switched at birth or something?"

Charlotte laughed out loud. Bernice's ears perked up and she opened the door a little wider. "No, the age difference just has a lot to do with the way we were raised. Since I was almost out of the nest by the time she came along, she was raised like an only child."

"Well then, so were you."

"Yeah, but you know how it is with the baby of the family. She was so spoiled."

"I never spoiled my kids. Dakota, my middle child, seemed to have inherited more of my genes. We understand each other. I think a lot of different factors played into my oldest son's change of personality, one of which is his uppity wife. As far as my youngest son is concerned, he's just a fence sitter. Wishy-washy to the end."

The friendly musings between the two women continued as they talked about their lives, the people in them and pyramids. Bernice wasn't able to hear the conversation but the laughter was loud enough to get her stomach churning. She was feeling like a third wheel and that her friendship with Grandy waning. The more she listened, the faster her heart beat. Soon her blood felt like it was boiling in her veins. She placed a cold washcloth on her forehead.

The new found friends continued their chatter up I-5 for a few hours before stopping at a Wal-Mart in Redding, California.

"Hey, Old Woman." Grandy hollered at Bernice, knowing she would not want to miss out on a trip to Wal-Mart. There was no response.

"I'm gonna open up a can of SPAM. Go see what's keeping your sister. She's probably doing her nails again."

Charlotte opened the door to the bedroom to find her sister sitting on the side of the bed gasping for air. "Are you okay?" asked Charlotte.

Bernice could not speak.

"Grandy, we need to call 911! Something's wrong with Bernice!"

Grandy came to the door and looked at Bernice. "Get her a paper bag. She's hyperventilating again."

"I don't think so," it was evident by Char's expression that she was extremely frightened for her sister. She felt Bernice's pulse. "Her heart's racing a mile a minute. Call 911, now!" Charlotte dug an aspirin out of her purse and gave it to her sister.

Grandy quickly dialed 911.

"911 emergency."

"My friend is having a heart attack. Where's the closest hospital."

"Is she breathing?"

"Yes."

"Is she conscious?"

"Yes."

"What's your location?"

"We're in the Wal-Mart Parking lot in Redding."

"Stay there, I'm sending an ambulance. What does your vehicle look like?"

"Beige motor home, blue trim."

"Stay on the line, please, until they arrive."

Four minutes seemed like hours until the ambulance arrived. After checking Bernice's pulse and blood pressure, the paramedics decided to transport her to the local hospital. Charlotte rode with Bernice while Grandy followed behind in the motor home.

"You better be faking it, Bernie," Grandy muttered to herself as she tried to keep up with the ambulance. Rare drops of tears escaped from her eyes, slid down and filled up the canyons in Old Red's cheeks.

Chapter 21

Grandy pulled up next to the ambulance at Shasta General. Before she could exit the motor home, she was surrounded by several patrol cars, their lights flashing and sirens filling the warm afternoon air. The officers approached the vehicle cautiously, then ordered Grandy to come out with her hands up. Her arms full because of holding Ditch and hanging onto her oversized handbag, she grumbled a half-hearted effort to show her palms.

The senior citizen's appearance – red hair teased high by the wind, an outfit designed more for a rebellious teenager than a matronly grandma and a small mutt of a dog in need of a good brushing, sent a look of shock across the faces of the officers.

"What's all this about?" Grandy snapped.

"You were driving erratically and 20 miles per hour over the speed limit. Why didn't you pull over when you saw my lights?" asked a clearly upset officer.

"I was trying to keep up with the ambulance carrying my best friend, she needs me."

"You should have stopped and just explained what was going on, we would have escorted you."

"Yeah well, I didn't have time for that. Can I put my hands down? They're getting tired and I need to get inside the hospital to check on Bernie."

The circle of police officers looked at each other, re-holstered their guns and retreated to their cars. The senior officer gave Grandy one last warning, "Next time, pull over and let us know what is going on. You could have hurt someone the way you were driving."

"Hopefully, there won't be a next time." Grandy turned and hurried into the hospital.

At the front desk, Charlotte was trying to answer the necessary admittance questions for her sister. She said to Grandy, "I need Bernice's medical card - " Char stopped short when she noticed Ditch. "What is that dog doing in here? You can't bring him into the hospital."

"He's worried about Bernie."

"She's right, Ma'am. You'll have to take your pet outside," the receptionist said.

"Fine." As Grandy was putting Ditch in the Fleetwood, she noticed a piece of paper on her windshield. She plucked the ticket off the windshield and put it on a car parked next to the motor home.

She returned to the hospital front desk and dumped Bernice's purse contents on the counter. Charlotte proceeded to search for the medical card as Grandy sat in a chair in the waiting room. Just for something to do, she asked a middle-aged woman what was wrong with her. While she was explaining her situation, Grandy got up and walked back over to the desk. She pushed her face through the opening in the glass partition. "I need to talk to my friend. What room is she in?"

"As soon as they get her settled, we'll call you and you can go see her. First I need to get some information."

"Her sister has been giving you information for the last ten minutes. What else do you need, her whole life story."

"As a matter of fact, we do need as much medical history as possible on a patient," the young receptionist said sternly. "Do you have anything you can tell us? Charlotte says the two of you have been traveling together the last few months."

"Yeah, Bernie is always constipated, is overweight, fusses too much and paints her fingernails twice a day. Anything else you want to know?"

The receptionist looked at Charlotte but all Bernice's sibling could do was shrug her shoulders.

Turning her attention back to Grandy, the receptionist said, "No thank you, I'll make sure I write your comments in her chart."

"See that you do that and tell the doctor he'd better fix Bernie better than new or else."

The disgruntled redhead then sat back down in the waiting room and challenged a little boy for a position on the armrest.

After the paperwork was completed, Charlotte sat next to Grandy and whispered, "I sure hope Bernice is going to be okay."

"She's probably exaggerating the whole thing. Everything is a drama to Bernie."

"I'm not so sure about that, Grandy. Her lips were turning blue and her blood pressure was way too high."

"Well, I need to go call Dakota. It doesn't look like we're gonna make it to Seattle by tomorrow. I wanna make sure I don't miss him."

"Didn't you just see him?"

"I'm just looking out for my grandson. I gotta see for myself what kind of person this Skye is."

"And what are you going do about it, Grandy? He's a grown man. He's allowed to make his own choices."

"Hmmf. You sound just like your sister."

"Maybe so, but I know I'm right about this one. My folks didn't approve of my husband Rich, and we were happily married for over 50 years."

"Why didn't they like him?"

"Because I was their daughter. And it's the same with you. Dakota's your son, and nobody is going to be good enough. My advice to you –"

"Excuse me, Ma'am," a nurse approached the two seniors. "You can see Ms. Gibson now."

Charlotte and Grandy followed the nurse down the hall. Bernice's breathing had calmed somewhat, but the monitor still showed a slight elevation in her blood pressure. She had been given oxygen and an IV was hooked to her arm.

"Hey, Sis." Charlotte softly touched Bernice's hand. Bernice opened her eyes and smiled at her two traveling companions.

"What'd they say? You gonna live?" asked Grandy.

"I'm sorry, Grandy. I know you wanted to get to Seattle by tomorrow."

"So you're not gonna live?"

"I didn't say that. The doctor wants to keep me overnight for observation."

"What do they plan to observe, Bernie? Your moaning and groaning?"

A look of hurt started to spread across Bernice's face until Grandy smiled at her, gave her shoulder an affectionate pat and said, "Just kidding, Bernie!"

"Oh Grandy," her friend said feebly, "you sure are a pain in the rear."

"I know it. Now, rest so that we can sneak out of here later tonight."

"Grandy! She has to do what the doctors tell her. There will be no leaving this place in the middle of the night."

Charlotte settled into a chair and gave Grandy a command. "Go call Dakota and take care of Ditch, I'll keep an eye on Bernice until morning."

Grandy looked over at Bernice, "middle of the night escapes are fun, aren't they, Bernie?"

"Yes Grandy, they are." She smiled and closed her eyes.

Chapter 22

Charlotte uncurled her body from the chair and looked at the clock. Bernice slowly turned her head and opened her eyes.

"What time is it?" she asked, her voice sounding like sticky tar.

"It's just past eight. How you feeling?" Charlotte gently brushed her hand across her sister's forehead.

"I gotta pee."

"I'll go tell the nurse. Maybe she can tell us when the doctor will be in."

"Where's Grandy?"

"She spent the night in the motor home after her failed attempt to commandeer another hospital bed."

"Are you sure she's still in the parking lot? What if she got mad and left?"

"I doubt it, Bernice. Grandy may be a bit unbalanced, but she's not that mean."

Bernice mumbled as she tugged at her pale blue backless nightgown, "You don't know her very well."

"What did you say?"

"Never mind."

"Here's the remote in case you want to watch TV. I'll be right back."

"Well, please hurry up. I really need to pee."

A minute later as Bernice was flipping through TV channels, Grandy entered the hospital room. She was wearing jean shorts, a lime green shirt with an alien face on it and matching alien earrings. Hanging from her arm was one of her many huge handbags.

"You ready to leave, Bernie?"

"No, I need to go pee. Charlotte went to find a nurse."

"You don't need a nurse, I'll help you. Just a minute." Grandy gingerly set her purse on a chair, reached inside and pulled out Ditch. She set him at the end of the bed. He promptly scurried close to Bernice.

"I'm pretty sure you're not allowed to have a dog in the hospital." Bernice's voice was strict but she was lovingly petting the dog she once found annoying.

"Never mind about that, get your fanny out of bed and I'll help get to the toilet."

"What about these wires and tubes attached to me?"

"I'll disconnect them." Just as Grandy was reaching for the breathing tube, Char walked in.

"What are you doing, Grandy?!" Charlotte's hazel eyes were frantic.

"Relax, I'm just going to help Bernie to the bathroom."

"The nurse is on her way in, let her do it." A slight movement on Bernice's bed caught Charlotte's eye. "What's he doing in here? You're going to get us kicked out of here."

"I really have to go pee!" Bernice said shrilly.

Apparently the old ladies' raised voices carried into the hallway, because a nurse appeared instantaneously.

"Hey Ladies," the 50ish nurse said, "you having a par-." She didn't finish her sentence when she saw the dog on the bed, Grandy's neon shirt and the patient sitting with her pasty white legs crossed. The nurse quickly regained her composure then ordered, "Everybody out except the patient."

"But -," Charlotte started to protest.

"Out! I'll let you know if or when you can come back in again. Except for the dog of course, you need to take it out of the building."

Grandy and Charlotte left Bernice's room, a pout on Grandy's face and a look of disgust on Charlotte's.

"I told you not to bring that mutt in here, now we can't be with Bernice," Charlotte said in anger.

"I'll take him back to the motor home then. What a bunch of uptight people around here," Grandy said as she marched towards the exit doors.

Unsure what to do next, Charlotte wandered down the hallway looking for the cafeteria. Once she found it, she ordered a cup of tea and a bran muffin. She sat at a small table and silently began praying for her sister.

After her conversation with God and half way through the muffin, Grandy made a dramatic appearance. She was wearing an orange robe and using her purple wheelchair to get around.

"What are you doing, Grandy?" Charlotte asked incredulously.

"It'll be easier to get in Bernice's room if I look like one of the patients."

"You don't look like a patient from this hospital, you look like a escapee from the psych ward."

"I don't see you doing anything to get us back in Bernice's room."

"Why don't you join me for some breakfast and we'll go check on her in a little bit."

Grandy stood up and got herself a carton of orange juice and a hash brown patty.

Charlotte tried to think of a safe topic to discuss with her new friend so she asked, "Did you talk to Dakota?"

"Yeah. He said he's only gonna be in Seattle for a couple of days before he leaves again."

"Leaves for where?"

"Oh, him and Skye and Rain are driving over to Montana to look for a buried treasure."

"Buried treasure? Sounds like something we should try."

"I've been thinking that same thought. After Bernie checks out of this place we'll go treasure hunting with Dakota."

Charlotte arched her black dyed eyebrows at Grandy and said, "First things first, let's go see if we can get back in to see my sister."

* * * * *

It had been almost 45 minutes since Grandy, Charlotte and Ditch had been banished from her room. Bernice not only relieved her bladder, but wolfed down a small breakfast consisting of lukewarm oatmeal, dry wheat bread and apple juice. She was hoping to watch Bob Barker on *"The Price is Right"* show, but didn't know what channel it was on. Just as she landed on a program to watch, her traveling companions entered the room. Bernice didn't blink twice at Grandy appearance, by now she expected almost anything from her.

"How you feeling, Sister?" asked Charlotte.

"Much better. The doctor is supposed to be here anytime between now and 11. My luck he'll show up right in the middle of my favorite show. It seems like forever since I've seen Bob Barker. He is such a wonderful man, I can't believe I actually got to kiss him on the cheek, and-"

"Bernice," Charlotte said her name slowly and softly, "Bob Barker retired from *"The Price is Right"* show awhile ago. Drew Carey is now the host."

Several seconds of silence filled the room before Bernice left out a loud wail, "Nooooo! He can't retire!" She covered her face with her hands, her braless chest began to heave and heavy sobs leaked through her fingers. A warning buzz came from one of the machines hooked to Bernice.

"Nice goin', Char," Grandy growled, "now we'll be stuck here even longer because of that stupid TV host."

90

Char snapped back at the crusty senior citizen in the wheelchair, "Hey, I didn't know she was THAT in love with Bob Barker. Do you think I would have put my own sister in distress on purpose?"

Grandy's intense blue eyes stared at Char. "No, but hurry up and get a nurse or I'm going to pull the plug myself."

Chapter 23

When the same nurse, who earlier had sent Grandy and Charlotte out of Bernice's room, tried to shoo them out a second time, the ladies started to protest. But when a six foot, two inch doctor also entered the room and gave them a threatening look, they grabbed their purses and fled.

"Hello Ms. Gibson, I'm Dr. March."

"Oh, Bob!" Bernice wailed. "I can't believe he's gone!"

"Bernice," the nurse said gently as she touched her shoulder, "What's wrong?"

"Bob Barker is no longer host of *"The Price is Right"* show," The wailing patient continued her exaggerated gestures and facial expressions.

"You need to calm down or we'll have to sedate you Mrs. Gibson," the young doctor said as he put his stethoscope to her chest.

The upset patient immediately stopped her theatrics and looked up at the physician. She tried to compose herself and said in a less dramatic voice, "You can't sedate me, then we would be late getting to Seattle. Plus, Grandy would kill me."

"Nobody's going to hurt you, much less kill you. We'll make sure to keep those two ladies out of your room," the physician reassured Bernice as he looked at the nurse.

"No, I want my sister and my friend back in the room with me."

"I don't think that's such a great idea," Dr. March said as he continued to examine his frazzled patient. "I recommend you relax and maybe I'll release you later this afternoon."

Bernice thought it best not to argue, so she asked once again if her sister and friend could come back into the room.

"ONLY if you promise to let me know if they start to upset you," scolded the handsome doctor.

"I promise."

Grandy and Charlotte entered Bernice's room with subdued expressions. It was obvious that the nurse and Dr. March had spoken to them before allowing them to see Bernice again.

Charlotte immediately went to her sister's side, kissed her lightly on the cheek and said, "You feel free to rest as long as you need to, Bernice. Your health is far more important than a road trip, right Grandy?" Charlotte gave her new friend a look that meant "you better agree."

"Yeah, she's right, Bernie," Grandy said without too much conviction.

Bernice tried to lighten the mood. "Hey, don't you think we ought to call Chet? He might be worried about us."

"What are you planning on telling him, Bernie? That your system overheated because your nail polish doesn't match your purse?"

"How can you say such a mean thing? I'm not faking my symptoms, Grandy." Bernice was injured by her traveling companion's remark.

"Do you believe everything I say, Bernie?" Grandy then pulled her cell phone out of her purse and made the call to Chicago.

"K-TAZ Radio."

"It's Grandy." When Grandy used to call the station, she had to explain who she was and that Chet was expecting her call. By now she had them trained to put her straight through.

Chet picked up the line. "Ladies and Gentlemen, it's our traveling grandmas. Grandy, how's it going?"

"Not so good, Chet. Haven't seen anything lately except a hospital bedpan and melting Jell-O."

"The hospital? What happened?" Chet's voice went from jubilant to concerned.

"Oh, nothing. Bernie hyperventilated, that's all."

Charlotte grabbed the phone. "You're gonna upset her. Let me explain. You see, Chet, Bernice has this heart condition and it was racing so fast she couldn't breathe, so we called the ambulance and the doctor wanted to keep her here overnight. We pulled in yesterday afternoon. She's feeling better today."
Char's voice blew into Chet's ear like a hurricane, and for a moment he was speechless.

"Is that you, Charlotte?"

"It's me."

"Well, hi. Is Bernice able to talk on the phone?"

"Well - "

It was Bernice's turn to pull the phone from Charlotte's hand.

"Hello Chet," Bernice used the most pitiful tone of voice she had.

"Hey Bernice, how ya doin'?" Chet inquired.

"Oh, a little better, I guess."

"I hope your condition isn't serious."

"Oh, I'll be fine." Bernice blew out a long sigh. "Hopefully I'll be released this afternoon."

"Well, Bernice, you take care. The lines are lighting up. Lots of well wishers, no doubt. You up to taking a couple of calls?"

"I'm a little weak, but I'll try."

"Go ahead, Caller."

"Hey Bernice. Sure hope you feel better soon."

"Who's this?"

"This is Hilda over here in Arkansas. Wanted to let you know that if you put a heavy layer of Vick's Vapor Rub all over your body, it will cure any ailment you have."

"Thanks for the tip and the phone call, Hilda."

"Next is Dolores in Wisconsin," said Chet.

"Yes, this is Dolores in Wisconsin, and I heard if you take and give yourself an enema of vinegar and olive oil, or was it canola oil and vinegar; I'm not real sure, something like that. Anyway, try it. It's supposed to work wonders."

Bernice's thank you to Delores was barely audible.

"Your next caller is somebody you know very well."

Bernice's eyes lit up at first, but then she frowned, thinking it might be Dog Face.

"Mom? Are you alright?"

"Joyce? Is that really you?"

"Yeah, Mom. I called Grandy's cell phone but it keeps going to voice mail. Why didn't you call me?"

"Honey, You know Grandy hardly ever turns the phone on and I've been kinda out of it since they put me in here. I was gonna call you later today. How's my granddaughter?"

"Jackie's doing great. Buck is great. I'm great. It's you we're worried about."

"I'm going be just fine."

"Promise me you'll call me later and let me know what the doctor says?"

"I promise."

"Okay, then, I'll talk to you soon."

"I love you. Kiss Jackie for me."

"I will. Bye."

"Bye."

"Well, Ladies," Chet announced. "We're about out of time. We wish you well, Bernice and be sure and call us tomorrow and let us know how you're doing."

"I will."

"Bye for now."

"Bye, Chet."

Bernice looked satisfied as she handed the phone back to Grandy. For once all the calls were for her and not Grandy.

"Why are you looking so smug, Bernie?" Grandy asked.

"No reason."

"Get some rest, you're leaving this place this afternoon whether you want to or not."

Chapter 24

By Thursday afternoon, Bernice was back in the co-captain's chair of the motor home. All three ladies were silent as they continued north on Interstate 5.

"The doctor said I need my prescription filled right away," Bernice insisted.

Grandy mumbled as she, again, pulled into the Wal-Mart parking lot. "Let's make it quick, we've already lost a day and a half."

"The doctor said I should take it easy. Can you pick it up for me, Charlotte?"

"Sure, no problem."

"Oh, and I need some other things, too. I'll make a list." Bernice moved like a rusty robot as she walked back to the bathroom to check her inventory of toiletries.

"The doctor said your heart's fine. How 'bout we move a little faster." Grandy was about at the end of her patience.

Bernice returned and handed the list to Char, pointing at and giving specific instructions for each item. "Get the quick drying nail polish, not pink, but tangerine. And that's tooth *paste*, none of that gel stuff. And..."

"For Heaven's sake, Bernie, just give her the stupid list."

"Fine, here. Oh, and I want the real Depends, none of those generic ones."

Grandy opened the door and headed towards the store, Charlotte followed behind.

Bernice watched as her two traveling companions were out of sight. She picked up the cell phone and dialed Joyce's number.

"Hello."

"Hey, Joyce, it's Mom." Bernice's voice sounded deliberately shaky.

"Mom. Are you okay? When do you get out of the hospital?"

"Oh, I'm out, Honey. We're on our way to Seattle. Charlotte and Grandy are shopping, so I thought it would be easier to talk to you without all the commotion."

"Yeah, I heard her on the radio. What's up with that? Are you sure that's a good idea, with her Alzheimer's and all?"

"Oh, she doesn't have Alzheimer's. It was just a reaction to some medicine she was on. Can you believe that?"

"She doesn't have Alzheimer's? You mean, she's okay?"

"Yeah, she looks and acts great, like she's been to a fountain of youth or something."

"I'd love to see her again. Any chance you might travel this direction?"

"It's hard to say, Joyce. You know how Grandy is. We might head that way just because she heard of some little green men convention. I know we're going to the State of Washington first to meet up with Dakota and also look for Bigfoot."

"Bigfoot? Are you sure you should be traipsing around in the forest?"

"I didn't say I was going to follow that dippy redhead into the woods. Char and I will probably go shopping or something."

"It must be fun to have your sister back in your life. Bet you've had a lot to catch up on."

"Oh yes!" There was a slight pause before Bernice continued. "Although, she and Grandy seem to have a lot more in common than we do."

"Aunt Charlotte and Grandy?"

"Yes, I'm afraid so. But they're watching out for me, really, everything's good."

"What did the doctor say?"

"He gave me a prescription, told me to take it easy."

"Well, what did he say was wrong?"

"Just a little anxiety. He just told me to avoid stress as much as possible."

"And you're still traveling with Grandy?"

"I know, I know. I'm fine, really. Grandy is treating me just fine. She was genuinely concerned for me."

"Well, if you start feeling bad, you check yourself back into the nearest hospital and make sure they know what they're talking about. Maybe you should get a second opinion, Mom."

"I'll be fine. I've got lots of help."

"Keep me posted on how you're doing, and don't forget, we have an extra room here whenever you decide to come."

"I know. I'll call you next week."

"You tell Grandy to drive carefully."

Bernice knew if she tried to tell Grandy how to do anything, Grandy would leave her on the side of the road. But she appeased her daughter and answered, "I will."

"I love you, Mom."

"I love you, too. Give Jackie a hug for me and say hi to Buck."

"I will. Bye now."

"Bye."

Chapter 25

After a seven-hour drive from Redding, one pee-stop, and a good night's sleep, Grandy was raring to go. She whistled as she fried up some SPAM, onions and toast for herself and her passengers.

Charlotte had just returned from taking Ditch for a brisk, morning walk. She poured herself a cup of tea.

"Better go wake up your sister. Have I got another nifty surprise for you two."

"This won't be anything that will raise her blood pressure, will it?"

"Maybe. Just tell her breakfast is ready."

Bernice was already awake when Charlotte wandered back to the bedroom.

"Breakfast is – "

"Ready. I know, I can smell it." Bernice wrinkled her nose and threw on her robe. As she observed Grandy's chipper mood, she knew that Grandy had some bizarre plan she hadn't shared yet. Because Bernice had gone to bed before they pulled into the campground, she didn't know what plans had been made or even where they were.

"Are we in Washington?"

"No, just outside of Portland. Only three more hours to Seattle. We're making good time. I figure we can eat, then call Chet, then there's something I wanna see in Portland."

"Don't tell me. Crop circles," Bernice sat down at the table as her sister served her a cup of tea. "Thanks."

Grandy slapped thick slices of SPAM and diced onions onto half-burnt pieces of toast and plopped the plate in front of Bernice. She didn't reply to her friend's comment.

"Do we have any fruit?" asked Bernice.

"Take one of your stool softeners," Grandy said as she put the bottle next to Bernice's cup of tea.

Charlotte interjected, "You know, if you ate three prunes every day, you wouldn't need those stool softeners."

"I'm tired of prunes, I just want a doggone piece of fruit, like grapes or passion fruit. Why is it I get a lecture every time I do or say anything?"

"Calm down. Remember what the doctor said about your blood pressure." Char put her hand on her sister's shoulder.

Bernice took a couple of deep breaths and replied, "I remember what he said. He said I shouldn't hold things in. So that's what I'm doing. I'm speaking my mind. Getting it off my chest, so it doesn't make my blood boil and cause me another trip to the hospital." She picked up her fork and pushed the food around on her plate before setting it on the floor for Ditch.

"I'm done eating dead pig," Bernice announced. "I'm opting for something healthier, like an egg and wheat bread." She stood up and began digging through the cupboards and refrigerator for a choice more suited to her desires.

"O-kay." Grandy looked at Charlotte and they both shrugged their shoulders.

"So what is it you want to see in Portland, Grandy?" asked Char.

"Charlie, you're gonna love this. We're going to the Alien Museum. I picked up a brochure at the registration desk last night. Here, take a look."

The adventurous senior citizen marveled at the brochure, her hazel eyes wide. "Amazing."

"Yeah, real interesting," Bernice chimed in.

"Now, Bernice, be a sport. It'll be fun," Char added.

"And if you don't wanna go, I picked this brochure up for you. We can drop you off and pick you up after we're done."

"What's this?" Bernice looked through the brochure and then handed it back to Grandy. "Very funny."

"What is it?" asked Charlotte.

"It's the vacuum cleaner museum."

Charlotte and Grandy laughed.

"I don't know what's so funny about that."

"Does that mean you want to go there?" Grandy asked with a mischievous grin on her face.

"No, I'll just go to the alien museum. But just remember all the times I've gone along with you, when something comes along I really want to see, you two are going, whether you like it or not."

"Yes, Ma'am." Grandy stood at attention and Bernice a mock salute.

"Thanks for breakfast." Charlotte began to clean up the kitchen.

"Go put your face on, Bernie, then we can call Chet."

"Don't tell me what to do, Grandy."

At that moment Ditch looked up at Bernice and barked.

"You either, Mutt."

Chapter 26

A nigh noon sun seemed especially hot as Bernice walked a couple of steps behind her traveling companions to the alien museum. Her mood had settled into a quiet resignation of emotions. After years of an almost nonexistent relationship with Charlotte, her hopes for a close sisterhood bond were dissolving before her eyes. In the short few days they had been together, Char had forged a much stronger connection with Grandy.

Bernice clutched her white purse with the determination of a woman hell bent on a taking a stance for action. She raised her voice at her two chattering travel companions in front of her.

"Hey, Old Ladies!"

Grandy and Charlotte stopped, turned around and stared at Bernice.

"Just so you know, I've decided that after we leave this crackpot place, we're going to visit a real museum. One that represents culture, history and information more educational than somebody's drug induced fantasies, AND you will not make one single comment on what you think about it, or me. Is that understood?" Bernice's face was set in a firm display of seriousness.

A solemn glance passed between Bernice's sister and her friend before they erupted in deep throated giggles.

"Okay Bernie," Grandy said as she and Charlotte continued walking towards the museum.

If she had Grandy's brazenness, Bernice would have cursed or thrown an object at the two, but she didn't. It was then that Bernice realized she was a true lady and could contain her anger in a proper fashion. She would show them how a real woman should act.

A ten foot tall statue of an alien creature welcomed the visitors. Grandy was so enamored, she paid for all three tickets and told the cashier to keep the change.

"I think I'll just sit here and wait for you two." Bernice said as she found her way to a bench near the entrance.

"Oh, come on, Bernie. I didn't pay for ya to just sit there."

"I'll be along in a few minutes. I'm just a little tired."

"Do you need a paper bag or some of your pills?" Grandy asked impatiently.

"No, I just need a moment."

"Okay."

Charlotte sat down next to her sister and asked, "Are you sure you're going to be fine? I can sit here with you for awhile to make sure."

Bernice touched Charlotte's arm, "No, please go and check this place out. I'll catch up shortly."

"Okay, if you're positive."

"I am. Go."

Grandy and Charlotte headed off to absorb the displays of alien artifacts and newspaper articles dating back to the 1940s.

"Look at this Grandy. UFO Sighting in Portland, Oregon."

"Yeah, we should do more night driving so we can see one."

"What would you do if you really came face to face with an alien, Grandy?"

"Ask to go for a ride in his spaceship."

Charlotte didn't know how to respond to her friend's answer so she began reading from a display on abductions. "Did you realize that 2-4% of all people on earth have been abducted by aliens?"

"I bet the number is actually higher than that. Most people don't want to admit they've been in the company of non-humans."

Bernice found sitting by herself in an alien museum discomforting, so she decided to check out the gift shop. The store carried mostly books on UFO's and aliens, but there were a few items of clothing and other trinkets. She thought about picking something up for her granddaughter, but decided Jackie had enough ET objects given to her by Grandy. Her infant granddaughter deserved to have Victorian style lace outfits, handmade toys and pretty gifts like music boxes and jewelry.

The lonesome grandma lamented as she pulled a photo from her purse and drank in the image of Jackie and Joyce. Her mind then took a path to her deceased husband, Jack, and how she wished he was still alive. "You and I would be visiting our family right now if you were still here," Bernice said softly to herself. "I miss you, Jack."

* * * * *

One of the more unusual attraction at the alien museum was the Vortex. Grandy and Char stood at opposite ends of it facing each other. Grandy was taller than Charlotte. When they switched places, Char was taller than Grandy. There was a level on the side of the building to show that it was not an uneven surface. The two finally gave up trying to figure out this phenomenon that defies human logic.

Next on the agenda was a lecture about 17 aliens being held captive by the United States Military. The moderator showed a film and encouraged all interested parties to get involved in an international effort to free the aliens. After the meeting, Grandy and Charlotte signed a petition to free the aliens. Each attendee was also given a handful of signs and bumper stickers.

"I'm gonna stick around and talk to this guy for a few minutes. Why don't you go see what your sister's up to," said Grandy, "make sure she hasn't fallen down or something."

Charlotte nodded and left the old redhead at the lecture hall. She found Bernice wandering through the museum, reading some of the newspaper articles on display. When Bernice saw her sister walking towards her, she turned away from the article, not wanting Grandy to think she was at all interested. She then noticed Grandy was not with her sister.

"Where's Grandy?"

"She'll be along. She's talking to some professor. We just heard him speak."

"Don't tell me. He was abducted."

"No."

"Grandy was abducted."

Charlotte chuckled, "No, of course not. But did you know that there are 17 aliens being held captive right now by the United States Military?"

"Let me guess, Grandy is one of them."

The laughter from Charlotte escalated and she gave her sister a half hug. "My Dear, you don't believe that hogwash, do you?"

Bernice was startled at her sibling's response. "I thought you believed in all this as much as Grandy."

"I find it a rubber necking experience, but I draw my limitations on certain areas of the subject."

"Well," Bernice paused a moment, "I'm glad to hear that I may not be as much as a third wheel as I thought. Do you think Grandy's about ready to leave now?"

"We can go check. And by the way, you're never a third wheel, Sister."

The siblings walked towards the front of the museum when they noticed a commotion outside. Several picketers were holding signs and marching around the building, Grandy right in the mix.

"Free the Aliens! Free the Aliens!" they all chanted in unison.

"How are we going to get her away from here?" Bernice asked.

"I have an idea," answered Charlotte. She walked up to her red headed friend and said, "Grandy, I really want to see the crop circles before it gets dark and I overheard someone say that a new one has just been discovered a few miles north of here. Do you think we could head that way?"

Grandy stopped marching and thought for a second, "I guess so, my feet are starting to hurt anyway." She left the circle of protesters and headed towards the Fleetwood.

"Hey!" one the alien lovers shouted, "you forgot to leave your sign."

"I didn't forget," Grandy yelled back, "I'm going to mount it to the outside of my motor home. Take the message cross country."

"Cool," the guy responded.

"Oh no," Bernice said quietly to Charlotte, "we're going to be traveling around now in a giant tin can of embarrassment."

"It won't be that bad, at least we'll get lots of honks and waves. Might be a fun way to meet people."

"Fun? I'd rather have cataract surgery."

Chapter 27

A relaxing vacation in Hawaii was just what Avis believed he and his family needed. The nerve binding futile attempts at catching up with his mother needed to be put in a remote drawer in the back of his mind. There was also a more recent incident involving his daughter.

Avis and Liza settled into the posh leather seats of first class on Northwest Airlines Flight 4820. Their 11 year old daughter Augusta sat across the aisle from them. Avis noticed the first thing she did was put on iPod headphones. He knew there were two reasons for this; one, to be absorbed in the latest tunes of the day; and two, for the convenient excuse to ignore her parents. A half hour before the family left for the airport, Augusta had managed to dye her baby blonde hair with streaks of cornflower blue. The young "tween" knew she was in trouble but there had been no time for a re-dye job.

As was his habit, Avis, rubbed his hands over his eyes. Liza put her hand on his arm and gave him a smile. The tense attorney smiled back before turning his focus to whatever was outside the airplane window. He would try his best not to think of his mother until after their getaway. "Good luck with that one," he thought to himself.

* * * * *

After Skye had passionately kissed her husband Dakota, she sweetly hugged and kissed Rain.

"I have missed you both terribly," she said, tears glazing over her large brown eyes.

"And we have missed you very much also, Love," Dakota replied.

The family of three took time to enjoy a sun-saturated lunch at a quaint café in Seattle. They sat outside and filled their stomachs and minds with delicious physical and mental food.

When it was time to leave Washington and head for Montana, they piled into a well used 1990's Subaru Outback that Dakota had traded for his pickup. There was a small sadness when the old truck changed hands, but the car would be more comfortable and safer for the family. The all-wheel drive of the Subaru would provide the off-road traction they would need when it was time to follow the directions on their treasure map.

"How did it go with your mother?" Skye asked.

"Well, it's definitely a story worth telling. There was quite a bit of commotion when Avis and my dad showed up unannounced. Ma had to make a quick escape."

"Wow! Wish I could have been there; sounds like a day at an amusement park."

"No Honey, it's a good thing you weren't. My mother is having a difficult time understanding why you took off and left Rain behind."

Skye looked over at her husband and asked in a cautious voice, "How difficult?"

"She's been trying to find a new mother for Rain." Dakota bit his lips and hastily continued, "Don't worry, Love, I think I have her convinced that you are a perfect wife and mother."

"I should have never told you not to tell her about my trip to Wyoming. I'm sure your mom would have never said anything to anyone. I was just so scared something would go wrong and Mr. Jerk would find out."

"Rescuing your sister from an abusive situation was extremely important, Skye. And it was even more important that her husband didn't know about the plans. My mom didn't need to know what was going on; we can tell her about it later."

"Do you think she'll forgive me?"

"I'm sure she will, once it is all explained to her."

"I hope so; I sure don't need to be replaced by a woman your mother picked out. No offense Honey, but Rain could end up with a mother who wears a metal strainer on her head."

* * * * *

A loud obnoxious knock woke Blackie from an afternoon nap. She shuffled to the door and opened it. Lester stood before her holding a large tattered Charmin toilet tissue box in his arms.

"Hey Gorgeous, long time no see!"

"What are you doing here, Lester?" Blackie's voice was clearly not welcoming her father-in-law.

"Why, I've come to see my favorite son and his wife."

"Howard's not here, he's working."

"That's okay, I'll wait for him." Lester shouldered his way past the angry barely pregnant woman, made his way to the livingroom and dropped his box on the floor. It immediately split open and dirty wrinkled clothing spilled out of its seams.

"Whoops, sorry about that," Lester said, "guess I should have used a garbage bag."

"Guess you should have," Blackie said, her unfriendly manner clearly not disturbing Lester.

"I'm kinda hungry and thirty, you gonna offer this here tired traveler anything for his gut?"

"You can get a beer from the refrigerator and I'll fix you a peanut butter sandwich. Supper is at 6 tonight."

"If you have any sardines to put on the sandwich, it would sure put a smile on this old man's face."

Blackie tried not to gag as she thought of sardines on peanut butter. When she composed herself she said, "We don't have any sardines, I could put a leftover pork chop on it."

"That would be just fine Darling, now, where's the T.V. remote?"

110

Chapter 28

Grandy's demeanor changed form jubilant to sullen as she turned off her cell phone. Even though the ladies had reached Seattle with what they thought was time to spare, Dakota, Skye and Rain had already left for Montana. She also noticed the evening was quickly morphing into a chilly night.

"We need to find a campground, Girls. In a couple of hours we can head out to the woods, start looking for Bigfoot."

"How do you expect to get from the campground to the woods, Grandy?" Bernice asked.

"Taxi cab." Grandy looked at Charlotte. "Do you have camouflage to wear?"

Charlotte hesitated a moment before answering, "No, I don't. I'll have to wear jeans and tennis shoes."

Mortified, Bernice said, "You are not going hiking around in the forest in the middle of the night! It's not safe."

Charlotte gently patted her sister's back. "I'll be fine, Bernice. I have faith Grandy will take good care of me."

"Yeah, Charlie will be fine."

"Do you even have any idea where you're going or what you'll do if you actually encounter a Bigfoot?" Bernice's voice was full of exasperation and concern. Her mind was cranking in overdrive trying to think of a way she could convince Grandy and Charlotte to not travel into the unknown. She decided to try different avenues of persuasion on Grandy. "What if I have another episode and need a doctor?"

"I'll leave the cell phone so you can call 911."

"What if you get lost and need the phone to call for help?"

"I've got a compass, we won't get lost."

"What if you get killed by Bigfoot, what do I do with Ditch and the motor home?"

"Keep Ditch, give the motor home to Dakota."

111

Bernice was fast running out of ideas to keep her sibling and friend from exploring the wilderness. She gave Char a pleading look of desperation. Charlotte just shrugged her shoulders.

Finally Bernice blurted out, "I'll make you a deal, Grandy. If you and Charlotte don't go out tonight, I promise to never complain about anything again."

Old Red looked at her friend with a small curve of a smile, "Don't make promises you can't keep, Bernie. Now, make some peanut butter sandwiches for me and Charlie while I find a campground for us to stay at. And pack a can of SPAM, Sasquatch might be hungry."

* * * * *

It took longer than expected to find the campground, register and park the motor home. The excitement of searching for Bigfoot had Grandy so wound up she almost ran over the neighboring campsite fire pit.

Once the water and septic were hooked up, Old Red walked to the campground office and asked about a cab. The accommodating caretaker said he would call for one and asked what time she wanted it to meet her.

"Charlie and I will be ready to leave in about 15 minutes, we'll meet the cab here." Grandy started to leave when she noticed a rack of postcards. She picked out three of them, each one a different interpretation of Bigfoot. After tossing a dollar on the counter she asked, "how many different families of Sasquatch are there?"

"What?" The campground caretakers looked at Grandy with confusion.

"You have three different pictures of Bigfoot, does that mean there are three different families or are they all related?"

For lack of a better answer, they said, "we're not sure, we buy the postcards from a traveling distributer."

"Well, next time you get postcards, ask, I'd like to know who I'm dealing with."

Chapter 29

Bernice gave a silent prayer of thanks as Grandy entered the motor home. In the few minutes it had taken her to walk back from the campground office, it had started to rain. The drops were fat, heavy and leaving the sky like a waterfall.

"Dang it!" Grandy said angrily, "Now we have to put off our trip until tomorrow night." She grabbed Bernice's sweater from the couch and wrapped her red wet hair in it.

Bernice was about to make a comment but it seemed like a waste of breath. Besides, there was a more important conversation she wanted to have with Grandy.

"Grandy, since you and Char aren't going out tonight, I thought we could talk about tomorrow."

"What about it?"

"I have it all planned out."

Grandy's blue eyes stared at her friend's determined face. She pursed her thin lips as she remembered the threat Bernice made the day before about doing something normal.

"Tomorrow we are going to go shopping and have lunch at a really nice restaurant along the water. Then in the afternoon we are going to a regular museum." Bernice's voice quivered as she tried to sound sophisticated.

"What's a regular museum?" Grandy inquired.

"The opposite of an irregular museum," Bernice retorted.

"Are you paying? I paid yesterday," replied Grandy.

"I know you did. and whatever it costs will be worth it, if I don't have to spend the day looking at spaceships."

After Grandy sent Char to cancel the cab and she took Ditch for the fastest potty break ever, the ladies settled down for the night. Bernice slept soundly, the next day's events cushioning her mind like down feather pillows. Char tossed and turned on the pulled out sofa, wishing she had an air mattress to soften her protruding bones. The one with the sweetest dreams though, was Grandy, conversations between herself and a Bigfoot floating through her mind.

* * * * *

It could not have been a more perfect morning. The sky was a brilliant blue and cloudless. Charlotte could hear Grandy singing in the shower as she returned from her morning walk with Ditch. Bernice, dressed in a melon colored, seersucker pant suit, was fixing herself a cup of tea. Charlotte popped her yoga DVD in the player and turned on the television.

"You don't mind, do you?"

"Not at all. Grandy might, but I really don't care. It's my day and I am not going to let her ruin it."

"'That's my girl. You really should try some yoga."

"You go ahead. It hurts just to watch you."

Grandy entered the kitchen wearing a pair of camouflage shorts and dark green T-shirt with a silhouette of Bigfoot along with the words "I Believe."

"I said we're going to a nice restaurant. You can't wear that," Bernice said angrily.

"Watch me."

Bernice's expression immediately went to one of a resolute threat. Charlotte uncurled herself from an unnatural yoga pose and took Grandy by the arm. "I'll help you pick something out," Char whispered discreetly, "Let's try not to upset her today, okay?"

"I heard that. And nobody's going to upset me today, because it's my day."

With a sliver of respect for her elder, Grandy cringed, but allowed Char to choose her outfit. To accent her tan slacks and white shirt, Char tried to loan Grandy a pair of earrings.

"Oh, no. That's where I draw the line. Unless you let me wear those ones you got at the Bone Room."

"Are your ears pierced?"

"No, but I could pierce them myself."

"I bet you could, but let's not."

"Oh, come on. It couldn't hurt any worse than getting a tattoo?"

"Yeah, but... you might get blood all over your white shirt. You look fine without earrings. Now behave yourself while I get ready to go."

Grandy went into the kitchen while Charlotte got dressed.

"You look nice, Grandy."

"Yeah, well, don't get used to it."

"I'm excited about today."

"That's great. How long is your sister staying with us?"

"What's wrong? I thought you two hit it off."

"We were until she decided to pick out my clothes. Now she's getting on my nerves."

"Oh, and you don't get on anybody's nerves?"

"That's a dumb question."

"She said it would only be for a little while. Can't you just be happy for me I get to spend some special time with my sister?"

Before Grandy could respond, Charlotte walked in. She noticed an uncomfortable exchange between the two friends.

"What's the matter?"

"Nothing," said Bernice, "Grandy's just being Grandy."

"Your sister was just wondering how long you'd be traveling with us," Grandy said, flashing Bernice an evil eye.

"I was not."

"Ladies, we have a beautiful day ahead of us. Let's have a vigorous walk to town for our planned activities."

Not feeling up to an argument, Grandy and Bernice gave each other a look of truce. Grandy fed Ditch, locked up the Fleetwood and grabbed her immense gunny sack purse. To the average passerby, the three seniors looked like kind, harmless grandmas. If they only knew.

Chapter 30

"Now, Grandy, you have to admit, you had fun today, didn't you?" Bernice, smiling like an overpaid teenager, stepped forward to hug her friend.

"It was alright. Too many ordinary attractions. Who cares about a smelly fish market or Bagel Universe."

"What about The Space Needle? Not every city has one of those."

Grandy used a nanosecond to reflect. Well, that was okay, but with hundreds of humans always around it, when do our friends from other planets get to use it?"

Char bit her lip to avoid a burst of laughter. In a few short days she had developed a true love for her sister's friend. My how she would miss them.

"I'm hungry," Grandy announced. "Those cones, or scones, or whatever they were, sure didn't fill me up at lunch." She began opening cupboard doors scrounging for a can of something to satisfy her growling stomach.

"Me, too," Char added. "I could even go for one of your SPAM concoctions you've been bragging about."

"Don't fix me anything, I'm just gonna have a piece of toast so I can take my pills. I'm bushed." Bernice yawned.

"This is gonna twinkle your toes." Grandy said as she started preparing her famous SPAMaroni. Charlotte thought it best not to actually see what ingredients went into the food she was going to eat. It was time anyway to take Ditch for a potty break. Bernice's sibling loved the long walks as much as the mutt did. Boy, she ached inside knowing she would miss the dog as much as her sister and friend.

Disgust lined Bernice's stomach as she watched Grandy fill a small glass bowl with chunks of SPAM, cheese, cooked noodles and various other odds and ends. She desperately hoped her looney friend would forget about Bigfoot. In the past, Bernice would eat SPAM dishes; now she determined to consume food that didn't contain by-products or ingredients she couldn't pronounce. Tonight it would be a supper of toast, fresh fruit, and yogurt. Before heading towards the bathroom, Bernice gazed at Grandy and asked, "was the day really not any fun for you?"

In a rarely heard tone of voice Grandy kindly said, "it wasn't as enlightening as the alien museum, but it wasn't as bad as I thought it would be." Grandy then turned her back to put the casserole in the oven.

Bernice knew that was a huge compliment coming from her friend, so her canyon wide smile stayed on her face as she shuffled to the back of the motor home.

Char returned a while later with Ditch just as Old Red was sticking her finger in the hot dish for a taste.

"Smells good."

"You're gonna love this," Grandy stated, as she piled a large helping of her famous dish onto Char's plate.

"Where's Bernice?"

"She's in the bathroom."

"Is she okay?"

"She's fine, probably painting her fingernails again."

"Well, I have something important to tell the both of you."

"Let me guess, you're broke and can't help pay for gas?"

"No, I'll tell you in a minute. I need to get Bernice in here first." Charlotte walked to the back of the Fleetwood and asked her sister to come join them at the table. An uneasiness assaulted Bernice's entire being.

"Don't ask any questions until I am done saying what I have to say," Char said in a firm voice. "These have been some of the most incredible days of my life, traveling with my beloved sister and her best friend. I can't thank you both enough for letting me ride along. But today, while the two of you were arguing over whether the motor home had room for a three-foot statue of Bigfoot, I remained outside the shop, people watching. Believe it or not, a handsome gentleman who looked a bit familiar walked up to me and asked if I was Charlotte Walker. I said yes I was. He said, 'I'm Henry. Henry Pond, we went to our high school prom together.' To make a long story short girls, Henry is also widowed, traveling the country by motorcycle and he asked me to go with him."

"You didn't say yes, did you?" Bernice's voice bordered on a meltdown.

"Yes I did, Sister. I'm ready for some romance and I've always wondered what riding in a sidecar would feel like."

"Who did he have in the sidecar before he asked you to go along?" Grandy's question was one less of concern than one of a possible mystery.

"He's an optimist, Grandy. He believed that during his adventures he would one day meet that special someone, and now he has."

Bernice had fallen into a sad silence, tears creating minuscule gutters through her makeup. Char hugged her tightly and said, "Please be happy for me, Bernice. I promise we won't let another 15 years go by before we see each other again."

"When are you leaving," Grandy asked as she shoved another forkful of food in her mouth.

"Tomorrow morning, early."

"Are we still going to look for Sasquatch tonight?

"I don't think so, Grandy. I need to pack and more importantly, I want to spend what time I have left with Bernice."

"Fine, me and Ditch will go then without you."

"Grandy?"

"What, Charlie?"

"It would mean a lot to me if you would stay here instead. I have a gift I want to give you."

"What is it? It better be worth me not seeing Bigfoot."

"It is, I promise."

Chapter 31

Ditch stood at the side of the bed, ball in mouth, staring at Bernice. The heat from his slightly sour dog breath is what finally woke the old lady.

"Grandy."

"What," was the groggy response.

"Your mutt wants to play."

"So go play with him."

"I don't have time, I'm going to spend every moment with Char before she leaves."

"Ditch." Grandy's furry friend trotted to her side of the bed. "Fetch." And the drowsy redhead threw the ball towards the front of the motor home.

"Ouch!" Charlotte squeaked as she touched her forehead where the ball had made contact.

Ditch barked like it was a game and scrambled after his toy.

Within two minutes Grandy and Bernice waddled their way to the table and sat down. Both were still tired from staying up until 2 a.m. visiting and playing cards with Char. The soon departing traveler set a cup of coffee in front of the sleepy eyed women.

"What time is it?" Grandy grumbled.

"Seven o'clock," chirped Charlotte.

"It's too dang early to be up."

"I'm planning on leaving within the hour, wanted to say my proper good-byes."

"Good-bye," said Grandy and she went back to bed.

A couple of sips of coffee and Bernice was fully awake, grateful she had this last hour with her sister.

"I'm going to miss you, Char. We should plan to meet at Joyce's place later this year for Thanksgiving or Christmas."

"I think that's a wonderful idea, consider it done."

During the next hour, the two siblings hugged, cried and said a thousand farewells. Henry showed up on his motorcycle and sidecar just as the ladies had exhausted their last minute instructions to each other.

"Tell Grandy thanks again for everything!" Charlotte shouted as she rode off with her new beau. "I love you, Bernice!"

"I love you, too!" Bernice yelled back. Her small puffy hand waved furiously until she could no longer see or hear her sister.

Back inside the motor home, Grandy had decided it was time to get ready to continue their journey. She was showering when Bernice entered the motor home. The unhappy grandma noticed the envelope from Char still laying on the counter. Inside was $5,000, a gift to Bernice and Grandy that Charlotte insisted they accept. Bernice tried to return her $2500 last night but lost the effort.

"This is my way of apologizing for not going on the Bigfoot quest with you," Charlotte had said to Grandy concerning her half. "Apology accepted," Grandy had replied without the slightest move to give back her share. Bernice was appalled that her friend would not even make a gesture to return the money, but then again what would one expect from Grandy.

Bernice tucked the money in her purse until she could think of a good hiding place. She then attempted to set aside her heavy heart by making breakfast. Bacon aroma filled the motor home. Eggs were transformed into mouth watering omelettes and toast absorbed thick slices of butter.

Grandy was done with her personal hygiene for the day, so she sat down by the table for the second time that morning.

"What's wrong with you?" Grandy asked.

"Nothing, you're not the only one who knows how to cook."

"You gave up bacon and all that other good stuff. Dry toast is your idea of a breakfast feast."

"Well, I thought I'd get off the same merry-go-round and eat something different today. Is that okay with you?" Bernice's voice was altering to the sarcasm mode.

"You can eat whatever you want as long as you don't end up in the hospital again or end up with a bad case of gas."

"Always the optimistic one, aren't you Grandy? Can't you ever look on the positive side of things?"

"I do. I'm positive your gastronomic system will declare a war and I'll be the loser during the battle."

Chapter 32

"Wake up, Bernie! We're at the center of the universe?"

Bernice rubbed her eyes and wiped the drool from the corner of her mouth. After that morning's gut bomb breakfast and exhausting emotional scene with Charlotte, her body demanded a midmorning nap.

"Where are we?"

"I told you, we're at the center of the universe."

"I heard you. Where's the center of the universe?"

"Wallace, Idaho. We're gonna stop here and eat." Grandy parked the motor home in front of a large, two-story brick building.

"I'm still full from breakfast."

"You can drink a glass of water then. I'm hungry."

Bernice read the sign on the building. "Oasis Bordello. I don't think this would be a proper place to eat."

"Splash some water on your face, I'm gonna take Ditch out to pee. Then we can walk over there." Grandy pointed down the street to a small café.

Bernice went into the bathroom and looked at her frazzled hair in the mirror. The right side of her face was red and creased from leaning against the window. She held a cool, damp washcloth against her face before applying another layer of powdered makeup. For a final touch of vanity Bernice carefully covered her lips in Dark Wine lipstick. As she smoothed her skirt one last time, Bernice wondered what kind of event she and Grandy would encounter next. Her off-base friend seemed to talk a little less about UFOs, and Bigfoot didn't usually travel eastward. That got Bernice wondering what mythical creature would become her friend's next obsession. One thing was for sure, Bernice desperately hoped her friend had forgotten about her scooters.

Retrieving them would probably mean an encounter with Dog Face, a person Bernice would be happy to never see again.

The ladies were the only patrons at the Blue Plate Tavern. The lunch crowd was long gone, and it was still a bit early for supper. The floral oil cloths and the small vases of flowers on each table reminded them of *The Passage of Time* dining room decor.

"Be right with you folks," an elderly, coal black haired waitress hollered from behind the counter.

Grandy turned to Bernice. "That waitress's hair is sure black for as old as she is. It doesn't look right, she shouldn't dye it."

It took all Bernice had not to laugh out loud at her short-sighted friend. Currently, Grandy's hair resembled a collage of colors randomly tossed together like a mixed red cabbage salad.

"I'm not hungry," Bernice said changing the subject.

"You already told me that," Grandy retorted.

The female travelers sat down and began eying the menu.

"What can I get you ladies?"

"Well, Flossy," Grandy read the waitress' name tag, "I'll have a double cheeseburger, an order of fries, an order of onion rings, and a beer, whatever you have on tap." Grandy smacked her lips.

"I'll just have an iced tea," said Bernice.

"No fries for you, Honey?"

"I'll just have a couple of hers."

"We'll see," Grandy quipped.

Flossy hollered the order to the cook and prepared the drinks for her customers.

As the ladies sat gazing out at the quaint little town of Wallace, a white-haired, balding gentleman entered the café. He wore a peculiar looking western shirt of purple and pink paisley material with matching sequences on the collar and cuffs. The man walked behind the counter and grabbed Flossy from behind and kissed her on the lips. He then turned and noticed the two patrons waiting for their meal.

"Oh, sorry. I didn't know you had customers." The man ambled over to Grandy and Bernice. He extended his long arm to offer a handshake.

"My name's Bud. That's my wife, Flossy. Welcome to Wallace, Idaho."

"My name's Bernice and this is my friend, Grandy. We're from Minnesota."

"Minnesota. Flossy's from Wisconsin. I'm from South Dakota." Bud gave the two women a puzzled look.

Bernice touched her face as if there was something to remove from it.

"Say, are you Grandy and Bernice the traveling grandmas from the Chet Baxter show?"

"Why yes we are," Bernice said proudly.

"Land's sakes, we listen to you every morning! Can I get your autographs?" asked Flossy as she delivered their order.

"Sure!" Bernice responded with great enthusiasm. Grandy was too busy to speak, as she watched through the window a man on horseback amble down the road.

"Can I get a bunch of them for all my friends? You have got quite a fan club right here in Wallace."

Bud couldn't take his eyes off Grandy and Bernice. "It's funny how you hear someone's voice and you have a whole different picture in your mind of what they look like."

"So what did you think we looked like?"

"Well, for one thing, when Chet said you had red hair, Grandy, I had no idea he meant that it was really red."

"Oh, that all depends on what day it is," Bernice explained.

"And what about Bernice? Did you think her's would be as blue as it is?"

Bernice attempted to laugh along with the other three, but her hands immediately flew to her hair and began touching it, a gesture she subconsciously hoped would change the color. In an attempt to get everyone's mind off her appearance she asked, "Why do they call this place the center of universe?"

"Because it's exactly that, the center of the universe."

Grandy ignored Bernice's moment of ignorance and stared at Bud's shirt.

"Have you lived here long?" Bernice continued as she daintily sipped on her ice tea.

"No, only about five years. We traveled through here during one of our vacations. Thought it would be a nice place to retire. Flossy just works part-time to make a little spending money for our entertainment."

"So what is it you do for entertainment around here? I see you have a brothel." Grandy smirked.

"Oh, you saw the famous Oasis. They went out of business long before we moved here. As a matter of fact, back in the old silver mining days, the ratio of men to women was 200 to 1 and there were actually five brothels right here in Wallace. The Oasis is a great, old building. They say it's one of the few structures that survived the big fire of 1910."

"You didn't answer my question," Grandy said.

"Oh, yeah. Well, as soon as Flossy is off work in a couple of hours, we're going to a hoedown just over in the next county."

"Hoedown?" Bernice's face revealed confusion.

"Square dancing, Bernie."

"Yeah, it's a hoot. Flossy makes all our outfits. Matching shirts and dresses."

"That explains the shirt," Grandy replied.

"My Flossy, she's pretty clever. You should see some of the outfits she's made for us."

"That's okay, we need to get going. My son and buried treasure are waiting for us in Montana," Grandy said.

After Grandy scarfed down her food and Bernice had drained her glass, the ladies signed several pieces of paper for their fans. Bernice's signature showed attention while Grandy just scribbled as fast as she could. After goodbyes and the purchase of a bumper sticker, the two travelers returned to the motor home. Ditch was taken out for a chance to pee, then the ladies left the parking lot with the Fleetwood tires spitting gravel until they reached the paved road.

Chapter 33

Through the motor home windows, the sun felt warm and lazy. The rays laid heavy on Grandy and Bernice's eyelids. Just as the grey haired grandma was sliding into a nap, the Fleetwood jerked, jumped then began an agonizing slow tip on its side. Both occupants opened their eyes as wide as their sockets allowed, followed quickly by closing them tight. They yelled as the motor home landed on its side with a metal scraping thud. It took several moments before the noise of falling objects, Ditch's yelping and the women's screams subsided. After an eternity of silence the ladies dared to survey their predicament. The coach was laying on its left side against an embankment. Grandy's face was pressed against the door window and her legs seemed to be twisted together. Bernice hung suspended from her seatbelt, her right arm hanging limply across her stomach.

"Ohhh," Bernice writhed in pain, "my arm really hurts. Grandy, are you okay?"

"I can't move my leg."

It was obvious Grandy wasn't going to get her door open so she unbuckled her seat belt and tried to untangle her legs. The pain was too excruciating so Grandy had to stop any movements. Ditch crawled on top of Grandy and began licking her face. "Not now, Mutt. Didn't you ever see *Lassie*? Go get help."

Ditch started to whine, his eyes traveling back and forth between his two companions.

"Atta boy, louder," Grandy ordered.

"I'd yell for help... but... I can't catch my breath. Oh, I just know we're gonna die," Bernice cried.

"Get 'hold of yourself, Bernie. We're no where near death. Try to open your window so we can crawl out."

"I can't, I think my arm is broke. And I have to pee." The injured senior citizen's voice broke into a high pitched sob.

"Oh great. Don't cry, Bernie, we'll be fine." Grandy's eyes searched for her cell phone. She saw it just out of reach in a corner of the dash. "Ditch, fetch the cell phone."

The shook up pooch whimpered softly and tried to snuggle closer to his owner.

"He doesn't know what you're asking of him," said Bernice.

"Give him a chance, he's still processing the command."

* * * * *

Minutes seemed like years before the ladies heard the sweet sound of rescue. Gravel popped beneath the tires of a vehicle that had stopped close to the Fleetwood. Within seconds Bud and Flossy, in their matching floral paisley outfits, poked their heads in Bernice's window.

"Are you okay?" a very concerned Bud asked.

"Do we look okay?" snapped Grandy.

"I think I broke my arm," Bernice moaned.

"I called 9-1-1 already. They should be here shortly. We'll stay here with you until they come."

"Won't you be late for your dance?" asked Bernice.

"There'll be other dances. We won't leave our favorite radio personalities until we know you're alright."

"We need to get out of here, Bud, open up that side door I need to crawl out and see the damage," said Grandy.

"Yeah, and I need to use a bathroom."

"Sorry, Ladies, I think it's best you stay put until help arrives. We don't want to risk any further injury to you."

Flossy then asked, "Is your dog okay?"

"He's fine, but I need to teach him how to fetch a cell phone."

"So what happened here, anyway? Did you see a deer or something?" asked Bud.

"Nope, just Bigfoot."

Bernice gasped, "you mean... you got us in this predicament because... you thought you saw Bigfoot?"

"I didn't think I saw Bigfoot... I did see Bigfoot!"

"It's possible," Bud replied. "There've been other sightings around here"

"Oh, Bud, Dugout Dan and three tourists on drugs don't count for reliable eye witness accounts."

"Now Flossy, you know hundreds of people have claimed to have seen Sasquatch," Bud lovely touched his wife's arm.

"Well - "

The sound of sirens interrupted the Bigfoot discussion.

"Finally!" Grandy said with frustration, "maybe once my foot is bandaged, the emergency guys can push my motor home upright and we can get to our next destination."

"I don't think so, Grandy. By the looks of things, this machine won't be going anywhere. It's pretty well thrashed." Bud walked around the wreckage shaking his head. "I sure hope you have insurance on this thing. It looks bad."

"Insurance is a ripoff. All I got is what the law required."

"What does that mean?" asked Bernice.

"It means you're out one really nice motor home. What a shame." Bud answered. "But, you're lucky to be alive."

"We didn't crash that bad," Grandy answered back. "One call to my brother Dog Face and he'll have this machine as good as new."

Chapter 34

Bernice stared at the cast on her right arm. She had opted for the black wrap thinking it wouldn't clash with her wardrobe. Now she silently berated herself for choosing such a depressing color. The only other injuries the frightened passenger sustained was a massive case of uncertainty and a few bruises. Thoughts of Grandy, the motor home and even Ditch expanded her brain to the point that she felt like it would start leaking out her ears. Meanwhile, her cramped body shifted, twisted and turned as she tried to get comfortable in a waiting room chair. Grandy's examination seemed to be taking far too long. Just as Bernice stood up to go look for her, an ample bodied nurse approached.

"Excuse me, are you with Ms. Wayland?"

"Yes, is she okay?"

"We are taking her upstairs for surgery. She broke her leg in two places."

"How long will she have to stay in the hospital?"

"I really don't know, Ma'am. You'll have to talk to her doctor after her surgery. It all depends."

"Do you have a phone I can use? I need to call my daughter in Texas."

"Of course, follow me. When you're finished you can wait in Ms. Wayland's room."

"Thank you." Bernice found Joyce's number in her purse. Her hand trembled as she dialed.

"Hello."

"Joyce, it's Mom."

"Hi Mom. Are you feeling better?"

"Well, I'm feeling pretty..." Bernice began to cry uncontrollably.

"Mom, calm down, I can't understand you."

"We had an accident."

"An accident? What kind of accident?" Joyce's voice went into panic mode.

"The Fleetwood is totaled, Joyce."

"Totaled? How did it happen? Are you okay? Where are you? Where's Grandy?"

"Grandy swerved to miss Bigfoot and the motor home tipped over. I broke my arm, but Grandy's going in for surgery, she broke her leg. We're in, in-" the sobbing slowed down as Bernice turned to the nurse and asked, "where am I?"

"Wallace, Idaho."

"I'll come get you, Mom."

"Oh, Honey. I hate to do this to you, I know you're busy with the baby and all."

"Mother. I'm coming to get you."

"Let me ask if they have an airport here." Bernice turned from the phone and spoke briefly to the nurse.

"Joyce, the closest major airport is in Spokane, Washington, but it's a little bit of a drive from there to here."

"Don't worry about that, Mom. You just stay right where you are, I'm gonna get a flight out tonight. See if you can get some rest and I'll be there as quick as I can. Did you contact any of Grandy's relatives?"

"Oh, I forgot all about them. I suppose I should try and get a hold of Dakota. I'll see if someone remembered to get Grandy's cell phone from the motor home."

"Just relax, Mom. Ask one of the nurse's to help you, I'm sure they will."

"Okay. I love you, Joyce, and I'm sorry."

"No reason to apologize. Just promise you'll take care of yourself. Don't worry. I'll be there as soon as I can."

"Okay. Bye."

"Bye."

* * * * *

In the few minutes it had taken Bernice to get back to Grandy's hospital room, she had forgotten all about calling Dakota. Instead, she crawled into one of the hospital beds and closed her exhausted eyes. Grandy's loud snoring woke Bernice an hour later. Her friend had survived her surgery, her leg bandaged and elevated. Except for her signature red hair looking like it had been teased by a comb belonging to the Abominable Snowman, Grandy seemed to be fine.

Bernice managed to fall back to sleep for another hour. When she opened her eyes, Grandy was attempting to take her leg out of the traction device.

"What are you doing!?" Bernice scolded.

"I need my cell phone, have to call Dog Face to come pick us up and fix the motor home."

"It can't be fixed, Grandy. It's over. Our trip is over. Joyce is on her way right now to come pick me up. I'm going to stay in Texas with her, Jackie and Buck," the words flowed out of Bernice's mouth fast and weighted with sorrow.

Grandy's blue eyes flared, "What are you talking about? I'm goin' back on the road, and so are you. You don't wanna move to Texas. It's hot and sticky and you won't get any sleep with that baby crying all the time."

"Grandy, be realistic. You had no insurance on the motor home. It's totaled. You're not in any shape to be driving anywhere for a long time. It's over."

"Bernie, stop being so negative. Dog Face can fix anything. By the way, where's Ditch?" Grandy looked around the room, the standard strength in her face and body fading with every gesture and comment.

"Flossy and Bud took him for a while. They have been so nice. They moved all our stuff out of the motor home and then had it towed," Bernice paused then said, "Grandy, I'm sure you'd be welcome at Joyce's if you want to come with me."

A sickening realization finally penetrated Grandy and she shook her head, "No." She viciously wiped away runaway tears. Then, just as quickly, she flipped a switch in her demeanor and said, "I don't want strangers pawing through my stuff. And Ditch needs to be here with me."

Bernice sighed, "I am sure Flossy and Bud will take good care of Ditch. You need to concentrate on getting well. And you need to start thinking about where you're going after you're released from the hospital. Are you sure you don't want to come with me?"

"No. Did you tell them not to give my dog any spicy food?"

"I'm sure your mutt is just fine. Now, let's talk practicalities," Bernice's voice was on the road to sternness.

"It's not over until I say it's over, Bernie. Get me the phone so I can call my brother."

Chapter 35

Chet Baxter arrived at the studio Monday morning at his usual time. Waiting for him was a message marked URGENT in bright red ink. He read the note then made a few phone calls. By the time he was ready to go on the air, his normally buoyant demeanor was wrapped in a dark shroud.

"Good morning, welcome to the Chet Baxter Show. I'm Chet Baxter and I'll be your host for the next three hours. For all our regular listeners out there, and especially those of you who are fans of the traveling grannies, I just received word that they will not be joining us for a while. They have met with a bit of bad luck. Bud and Flossie from Idaho reported to me this morning that Bernice and Grandy were involved in a terrible accident. Their motor home was totaled but thankfully, our celebrity grandmas are going to be okay – some broken bones, cuts and bruises, but they are both conscious and the prognosis looks good."

Chet continued, "I'll be doing something a little different this morning. I'll be opening up the lines for the full three hours to let you, the fans, call in with your well wishes for Grandy and Bernice. And Grandy and Bernice, if you happen to be listening, just know that we miss you and pray for your speedy recovery. We hope you'll be enjoying again soon the freedom of the open road. Now to our phones. Mike and Roseanne in Macon, Georgia, you're on the Chet Baxter Show."

"Oh, we are just sick about the accident. How did it happen? Is there anything we can do to help? We'd like to send Grandy and Bernice a card, is there an address where we can send it?"

"The information I have concerning the accident is limited. From what I understand, something ran in front of their vehicle causing them to swerve off the road. As for correspondence, if you send it here to the studio, I'll make sure it is forwarded to Grandy and Bernice. Our address is K-TAZ Radio, P.O. Box 8493,

Chicago, Illinois 60601." Chet repeated the address twice and proceeded to the next call.

"Hello, Chet. This is Lillian from the retirement home in Minnesota where Grandy and Bernice used to live. We are all so worried about them, do you have a phone number where we can call them?"

"I'm choosing not to give out their exact location or any phone numbers at this time. I plan to call the ladies later today and get any update on their condition."

For the next two and a half hours, calls were taken offering help, financial and otherwise. All of them conveyed to the injured travelers best wishes and a speedy recovery. The last call of the day was Roscoe, a fellow alien lover like Grandy.

"Hey there, Chet. This is Roscoe from the road. I'm a good friend of Grandy and Bernice. If you talk to them, would you let them know I'm in Nevada? I have a cell phone number I can give you to pass on."

"Stay on the line, Roscoe, I'll have my assistant get the number from you."

After Chet wrapped up his show, he sat back in his chair and bowed his head to pray. He had no idea that his morning chats with the grandmas had become so popular, or that the lives of these two ordinary yet extraordinary women had such an impact on the country.

Chapter 36

After wrapping herself in one of her husband's work shirts, Blackie grabbed the phone and quietly headed towards the back door. As she passed through the livingroom, Howard's wife glanced at her father-in-law Lester, sleeping on the couch. The old man's fat arms were stretched above his head, the white underbelly skin blotched with dirt. He was without shirt, his hairy mound of a stomach convulsing from deep, loud snores. Adding to the revulsion was drool pouring out the side of his mouth like a contaminated waterfall. Blackie shuttered with disgust and moved as far away as possible from Lester as she walked by. Once outside, she went and sat in their tire-free, rusty '69 Chevy pickup. Only after locking the truck doors did she dare call Howard.

"Hey, Babe," Howard said, "what's up?"

"It's your mother."

"What about her?"

"She's in the hospital."

Howard spilled his coffee on his lap as the news took him by surprise, "Oh, @#$! What happened?"

"According to the Chet Baxter show, she and Bernice were in an accident."

Genuine sympathy broadcasted from Howard as he began firing questions at Blackie. "Exactly what happened? How badly are they hurt? What hospital are they at? When did - "

Blackie impatiently interrupted her spouse's line of questioning, "I only caught the last few minutes of the show. I know it happened in Idaho and that's about all. You need to call Chet yourself and get more information from him."

"What's the number, Babe?"

Howard pulled his beer truck off the side of the road and wrote down the number.

"Did my dad hear the radio show?"

139

"No, as usual, he's sleeping the day away on the couch. You need to tell him to leave soon, Howard, or I'll pack my bags and go live with my brother."

"I know, it's just that my old man has - "

"Quit making apologies for him, Howard. He might be your father, but he is a lazy, lecherous excuse of a man. He's either gone by the end of the week or I am."

After ending the call with Blackie, Howard ransacked the glove compartment looking for something to clean off his pants. Finding only a crumpled napkin, he made a half-hearted attempt to wipe away the stain, gave up and threw the napkin on the truck floor. A spectrum of emotions now filled Howard's body – anxiety for his mother, annoyance with Blackie, frustration with his father and anger that the beer company he drove for didn't keep a stash of moist towelettes in the truck.

Howard took a deep breath before calling the K-TAZ radio station. He was disappointed to learn that Chet had left for the day and wouldn't be back until tomorrow. A woman with a pleasant voice assured Howard that she would give Chet his name and phone number.

"Another roadblock, great, just great," Howard grumbled.

Knowing he needed to keep on schedule with his deliveries, Grandy's youngest son eased his truck onto the road. In the back of his mind, was the nagging suggestion he should call his older brother, Avis. Not because he believed Avis really cared about their mom, but if Avis found out Howard didn't share the information he had found out about Grandy, there would be hell to pay. Reluctantly, Howard dialed Avis' cell phone and was secretly relieved when the voice mail answered. Howard left a message and hung up. Ten minutes later Avis called back.

"What's this about Mom being in an accident?"

"Well hello to you, too. How's Hawaii?"

"Never mind about Hawaii, what else can you tell me about the accident?" Avis' voice was clipped and business-like.

"Like I said in my message, I won't know more until tomorrow when Chet gets back to the station." Howard's irritation with his brother was clearly becoming apparent.

"I can't believe you aren't doing something right now." Avis' condescending tone created another defensive wall between him and his brother.

Howard's angry voice responded, "What am I supposed to do, Avis? I don't have the resources like you, to hire private investigators or just fly to an area she may or may not be."

With the tiniest effort to be more civil, Avis said, "I'll take the next available flight to Boise, Idaho. By tomorrow, I can find out exactly where Mom is and take another flight to whatever town she's in. I'll call you as soon as I know something."

"Whatever." Howard hung up without saying good-bye.

As soon as the brothers disconnected, Avis' phone rang again.

"Avis Wayland."

"Yeah, uh, this is Stormy."

"What do you want, you worthless excuse for a private investigator?"

"I think I found your mother?"

"Let me guess, she's in a hospital in Idaho?"

"Yeah," Stormy's was clearly surprised by Avis' answer.

"The whole country knows, you idiot, it was on national radio. Now if you can tell me which hospital she's in, I might consider hiring you again."

"Well, I need a retainer before I can do any investigative work."

"You still owe me, Stormy, for the major screw-up work you did a month ago."

There was a small pause before the P.I. replied, "You don't have to get nasty Avis. Tell ya what I'm going to do. When I find what hospital she's in, I'll give you the information for free."

Avis terminated the call, leaving Stormy to repeatedly say into his phone, "Avis, are you there? Can you hear me? Avis? Avis? Can you hear me?"

Chapter 37

Frustrated at not being able to make contact with Dakota, Grandy began flipping spoonfuls of cold oatmeal at the hospital T.V. screen. She was aiming for the *Price is Right* show's host, Drew Carey. It was midmorning, the day after she and Bernice had the accident. The old redhead should have been exhausted and resting, but Grandy's feistiness was a bigger volcano than her injuries.

Lying in the bed next to her traveling companion, Bernice kept looking at her watch, wondering when Joyce would be arriving. The two women had little to say to each other, since their future together was about as uncertain as a genuine extraterrestrial encounter.

A middle-aged, chubby nurse named Linda, entered Grandy and Bernice's room and frowned as she noticed the mess on the T.V.

"You know Grandy, if you didn't like your oatmeal, you could have sent it back earlier with the rest of your tray," Linda said in a mock scold.

"I'm bored and this is more fun than watching Bernice stare at her watch. Bring me my dog and I won't throw anymore slop."

"You won't toss anymore food anyway, Grandy, or I'll make sure you don't get fed tomorrow."

"I won't be here tomorrow," Grandy said adamantly.

"Grandy," Bernice interjected, "remember, you don't have a motor home anymore."

"I will have as soon as I get a hold of Dog Face. Hand me the phone, I need to try calling him again."

Nurse Linda rolled her eyes as she left the room to retrieve supplies to clean up the dripping oatmeal.

Bernice thought about telling her best friend one last time about the hopelessness of the Fleetwood, but decided it would be a waste of her breath. She instead handed the cell phone to Grandy and watched as she dialed Dog Face's number. Bernice silently prayed Joyce would arrive long before Grandy's sibling thought about showing up.

"Hello."

"Dog. Where have you been? I've been trying to reach you? You need to get over here to Wallace, Idaho, now."

"Idaho? What are you doing in Idaho?"

"Haven't you been listening to the Chet Baxter show? Bernie and I were in an accident. I need you to come fix my motor home."

"Is Miss Bernice okay?"

"Yes, Bernie is just fine, but I'm stuck in the hospital with a broken leg and I need to get back out on the road."

"How bad is Miss Bernice hurt?"

"She only broke her arm, now are you coming or what?"

"What happened?"

"I had to swerve to miss Bigfoot and the motor home lost control and tipped over."

"Wow, what did he look like?"

"Bigfoot, you moron. Did I mention I'm in the hospital?"

"How bad is the damage?"

"I said I broke my leg." With every question and answer, Grandy's annoyance thermometer spiked another degree.

"I know that, I mean the motor home."

"I don't know, a couple of people said it's totaled but I don't think it's as bad as they say it is. Just bring a hammer and some duct tape and whatever else you have in that toolbox of yours for fixing bent metal."

"Did you call the insurance company?"

"Won't do me any good, since I didn't have any insurance."

"You didn't have any insurance?" Dog Face's voice sounded incredulous. "Even I have full insurance on my old pickup."

"Dale Evans Krone! Get your butt to Idaho now! Avis I'm sure has heard about the accident and is probably on his way here now. You need to be here sooner."

"I can get there maybe by Friday."

"Friday! I'm out of here tomorrow."

Bernice whispered, "Now, Grandy, you don't know that."

"Watch me." Grandy grumbled at Bernice then continued her conversation with her brother. "I really need you here tomorrow."

"No can do. My truck is on the blink. Waiting for parts. And you know I don't fly. Besides, they won't let me bring my tools on the plane. Sorry."

Grandy gritted her teeth, her mind spinning, trying to find a way out of her predicament. She then yelled into the phone, "Then buy a bus ticket or take a cab. Just be here tomorrow." Before Dog Face could respond, Grandy disconnected the phone.

Chapter 38

By Monday evening, Grandy and Bernice's hospital room was filled with flowers and cards. Between Bud, Flossie and the hospital staff, word had spread quickly to areas surrounding Wallace, Idaho. Outside the hospital, beneath the grannies' window, a small candlelight vigil was being held. Chet Baxter, who had arrived from Chicago also in the first stages of night, had entered their room carrying an overflowing vase of orange/red Gerber daisies, red carnations, Irises, babies' breath and greens. His visit was bittersweet. Seeing the senior citizens felt like a reunion with favorite family members. It also threw a fire log on Grandy's determination to continue motor home travels. Despite her protests, it was finally decided the most sensible scenario concerning the talk show would be to put it on hold and resume if and when Grandy and Bernice returned to their cross country adventures.

Shortly after Chet left, Bernice was forced to give up the bed she had been resting in because of a new patient. Miss Emma Hayes had fallen and broken her hip earlier that day. She was in great pain despite medication designed to mask it. The 89 year old woman began to moan and call out for a nurse. After twenty minutes of the unpleasant sounds, Grandy could hold her tongue no longer.

"Hey, could you keep it down? My friend and I are trying to carry on a conversation here."

"Oooooh, it hurts so bad, oooooh."

"Try thinking of something else, like a hot, young male doctor, chocolate pie or a margarita." Miss Emma was reminding Grandy of Pauline, another moaner from the *Passage of Time Retirement Home*. Pauline's room had been right next to hers and Bernice's and Grandy had almost snuffed her out with a pillow.

When Tiffany, a 25 year old nurse, fresh on shift, came into the room, Grandy started in on her.

"You know, Bernice was here first, she shouldn't have to give up her bed."

"It's not technically her bed, Grandy. Bernice was treated and released. She's just been allowed to occupy the bed as a courtesy from the hospital."

"She shouldn't have to sit in an uncomfortable chair. Can't you roll another bed in here?"

"Sorry, Grandy, no."

The redheaded patient gave the nurse a look designed to intimidate her before continuing onto another complaining comment.

"Well, the least you can do is get the old lady to shut up. She sounds like a fight between a cobra and a mongoose."

A look of shock quickly swept over Tiffany's face. She looked at Grandy then at Bernice, unsure of what to say.

"Don't mind her," Bernice said, "she always talks that way."

"Miss Hayes is in a great deal of pain, Grandy, have a little compassion. I bet nobody complained when you expressed your discomfort," the young nurse said as she valiantly tried to soothe Miss Emma.

"I never sounded like a farting whistle."

After a sharp glance, Tiffany left the room. Grandy turned her attention to a T.V. show. After a few moments, she said to Bernice in a loud whisper, "I tried to be nice about the situation, apparently that doesn't work, so I'm going to Plan B."

Hesitantly, Bernice asked her loopy friend, "What is Plan B?"

Grandy held up a remote. "I've got Miss Emma's bed controller. Next time she starts wailing again, I'm going to give her a ride."

Chapter 39

Sold out flights to Spokane forced Joyce to fly into Boise, Idaho. The switch to a different airport was not really that much of an inconvenience, but Bernice's daughter was not happy that she would be arriving on Tuesday instead of Monday. She had called her mother the night before, explaining and apologizing for not being there when she said she would.

"Don't worry about it Honey, I'll be fine, you just be careful," Bernice had said, a barely noticeable shadow of disappointment in her voice. "By the way, how's my precious granddaughter?"

"Jackie is fantastic, Mom. You won't believe how much she's grown. I know she's as anxious to see you as you are to see her."

"Like I said Joyce, don't worry about me, you just get here when you can."

"Okay Mom, see you soon."

"Bye Dear."

Bernice hung up the phone and began to cry softly.

"Hey Old Woman," Grandy said, trying to sound rough, "why are you crying? Did you just remember your bottles of nail polish broke? Bernice's roommate began to snicker.

"Noooo, Joyce won't be here until tomorrow," Bernice sniffled.

"Are you that anxious to get away from me?" Grandy asked indignantly.

"No, I just don't want to be here when Dog Face shows up."

"Now, that's the dumbest thing I've ever heard a person cry about."

The tears in Bernice's eyes began to evaporate and she forced a soggy smile at her best friend. "Joyce will be here tomorrow to pick me up. Who's going to come get you?"

Grandy glared at Bernice and gave no response.

* * * * *

Midmorning Tuesday, Joyce found herself standing at a car rental counter at the Boise Airport. She was filling out the required paperwork to rent a car when someone tapped her on the shoulder. Startled, she jumped at the unexpected touch.

"Joyce?"

Bernice's blond-haired daughter stared at the middle-aged man who had spoken her name. It took a few moments before she realized who it was.

"Avis?" The shock of seeing him caused her to drop the pen she was holding.

"Yeah, what a coincidence, you must be on your way to see your mom?" Avis retrieved the pen and handed it to Joyce.

"Thank you."

A very tight knot quickly formed in Joyce's stomach as she tried to think of what to say to Grandy's son. She knew that over the last few months, her mom's friend had been desperately trying to avoid her eldest son. Her mind raced with several thoughts. Since their accident, had the relationship changed between the two of them? How could she possibly explain her presence in Idaho and how in the world could she lose Avis?

"Why, yes I am," Joyce said slowly. She turned back to the car rental counter to finish the paperwork.

"Look, I'm sure my mother has been saying quite a few unflattering comments about me, but I can assure you I am only looking out for her best interests. I really am concerned about her." Avis paused a moment before continuing, "Do you know which hospital they are in?"

"Of course I do, don't you?" Uncertainty was evident in Joyce's voice.

Avis ignored the question and asked one of his own," Why don't I follow you? I was just on my way to pick up my own rental car."

Short of making a scene that would involve security and a lack of proof for accusations, Joyce had little choice but to let Avis follow her.

Chapter 40

Bernice had spent Monday night sleeping on a couch in the waiting room. Sympathetic hospital staff had provided her with a pillow and blanket, but were not able to find an empty bed for her. There had been an offer for a free hotel room and also one vigilant fan member who offered the grey-haired grandma a bed at his house, but Bernice politely declined, stating she needed to be close to Grandy.

After an uncomfortable night on the sticky, vinyl sofa, Bernice went to Grandy's room. She tried her best to shower and get ready in the tiny bathroom. With a broken right arm, trying to do anything felt like a no-solution puzzle. Tears saturated Bernice's cheeks as she realized that it wasn't just the fact that trying to hold Jackie was going to be difficult; little take-for-granted tasks like pulling up her underwear were much tougher with only one hand. She was beginning to believe she would have to forego the Spandex girdle design and start wearing men's boxers. Painting her nails would be out of the question and a fresh order of tears made more streaks through Bernice's makeup.

Outside the bathroom door, Bernice heard Grandy and Emma arguing over television shows.

"Who died and made you queen of the telly?" Emma asked. She was obviously ticked off with her roommate.

"I was here first; besides, nobody likes watching those stupid reality shows." Grandy angrily responded.

"Reality shows are not dumb, they're interesting."

"No, they're not! It's not any different than a stupid soap opera. All those plastic-filled, anorexic floozies pretending to be in love with men who look and act like a 3D magazine ad for male enhancement." Grandy stared at Emma after her mini tirade.

Just as Emma opened her mouth to let loose a retort, a male nurse named Oscar entered the room, face flushed and hands on his hips." That is quite enough, Ladies," he said. "We can hear your silly squabble all the way down the hall. You are disturbing the other patients."

"She started it," Emma said in a barely controlled voice.

"I did not."

"It doesn't matter who started it," Oscar interrupted. "I'm ending it, now. Hand me the TV remote, I'm choosing what you two are going to watch."

"Better not be that ridiculous *ER* show, I'll miss my bed pan if you turn that on," Grandy's voice was like spoiled vinegar.

Oscar just gave her a stern look and proceeded to turn channels until he found *Animal Planet*. "Here you go, Ladies, enjoy, and next time I hear raised voices coming from this room, all TV privileges will be lost."

It wasn't until Oscar left the room that Bernice dared to come out of the bathroom. Her scared, silver eyes darted back and forth between her best friend and the patient who had taken her bed. She wasn't sure if it was safe to speak or move, so Bernice just stood there.

Grandy observed her traveling companion's uncertainty and decided it wasn't necessary to heap frustration on top of her fear.

"Hey Bernie, pull up a chair next to me, I need to talk to you."

Bernice drug a chair across the floor, the noise causing Emma to give the ladies a dirty look.

"Don't mind her," Grandy whispered, "she can't run faster than I can throw."

Once Bernice was settle in the chair, she glanced at her watch. She noticed Grandy intently observing her motion.

"What?" Bernice asked.

Grandy asked in a wary voice, "Why do you care what time it is?"

"Joyce is supposed to be here soon. I just want to make sure I'm ready for her."

"Hmmmf." Grandy stared at the TV screen, her lips pursing as she watched two kangaroos kick the crap out of each other.

"What did you want to talk about Grandy?"

There was no immediate response from the wound-up redhead. Bernice waited a few moments before speaking again. "Grandy?"

"What?"

"What did you want to talk to me about?"

"Nothing, you just looked silly standing in the bathroom doorway."

The two friends watched TV in silence until lunch was served. If it wasn't for the threat of having their only entertainment removed, Grandy would have created a fuss about the unrecognizable meal on her tray.

"How hard is it to create food that doesn't look like it's already been down the garbage disposal?" she muttered mostly to herself.

"It's not that bad, Grandy, the Jell-O is firm and the noodles are soft. Remember how it used to be the opposite at our retirement home?"

A long heavy sigh escaped the broken-boned redhead, "You know Bernie, I just can't stand the thought of being in a place like that. Maybe you should call Dog Face and beg him to come get me. I'm sure he'd drop everything for you."

To see her friend in a deflated and defeated attitude was almost more than Bernice could bear. Grandy was always the strong one, the ornery one, the one who could handle anything.

"Well maybe – " Just as Bernice was about to consider Grandy's request, Joyce came bounding into the room.

"Mom!"

"Joyce!"

The mother and daughter hugged tightly, grateful tears falling everywhere. After several minutes and the usual "how are you questions," Joyce walked to Grandy's bedside and gave her a hug.

"How are you doing, Grandy?" Joyce asked.

"How do you think? I need to get out of here. You didn't happen to see my brother in the parking lot, did you?"

"No, but – " Joyce stopped in mid-sentence, her face turned red and she looked at her mom helplessly.

"But what?" Grandy asked with alarm in her voice.

"Avis is here, he followed me from the Boise airport." The words tumbled quickly from Joyce's mouth. She then took a couple of steps backward and grabbed her mother's one good arm.

"He what!" Grandy shouted. Her blue eyes instantly became three shades darker and her red hair seemed to grow eight inches higher.

"I'm sorry Grandy, I had no way to get rid of him, and the meeting was purely accidental." Joyce's voice trembled.

This time Bernice raised her voice to her former roommate, "Don't you be mad at Joyce, Grandy, you know how sneaky your son can be."

It was only for a second that Grandy closed her eyes to regroup, when she opened them and saw Avis standing before her.

"Hello Mother, how you doing?"

"How do I look like I'm doing? First my motor home gets wrecked, my leg is broken and then you show up. How much worse can it get!" Grandy was back in a yelling mode which promptly brought Oscar back into the room.

"I told you ladies that – "

"Get this man out of my room, Oscar; he's here to kill me. Don't let the family resemblance fool you."

Oscar looked at the raving senior citizen and then at the calm, well-dressed man at her side.

"Mr. Wayland said he's your son and he is here to take you home," said Oscar.

"I'm not going anywhere with him, especially to his house, his wife bakes cookies that give people the runs."

It was obvious that Grandy was serious in what she was saying, but it took all Oscar had not to laugh out loud.

"I'm sorry Grandy, but the doctor is on his way to your room to talk about sending you home. Unfortunately, you can't stay here after you're released," Oscar said.

"Hurrah!" Emma injected.

"Shut up, Old Lady, before I –" Grandy wasn't allowed to finish her sentence because Bernice erupted in a new shower of tears.

"I, I, I'mmmm, going to miss you Grandy!" Bernice hobbled over to her friend and laid her head on her shoulder.

"Mom," Avis tried to speak above the wailing, "don't make a scene, you'll only have to stay with us until you are healed."

The chaos escalated as Bernice continued to cry, Avis argued with his mother, Emma cheered, Joyce tried to comfort her mom and Oscar tried to get everyone's attention by a weak whistle.

"Excuse me," said a voice not at the shouting level but fairly close.

Everyone stopped what they were doing and turned towards the voice. Grandy's doctor stood in the doorway, her petite stature suddenly a huge presence in the room.

Chapter 41

"Everybody out except Ms. Hayes and Ms. Wayland," Dr. Rachel Holland said in a commanding voice.

A unison of "but – " echoed through the hospital room. The protest went unheeded and the glare from Dr. Holland's eyes said, in no uncertain terms, that she was serious.

After the small group left, Dr. Holland went to Grandy's bedside, then picked up her arm to take her pulse.

"Your pulse rate is elevated Ms. Wayland, there is too much excitement around you. If you don't relax, I won't be able to release you tomorrow so you can go home."

"I've been told that my motor home is totaled. Until my brother from Minnesota gets here, I plan to camp out in this room."

Hearing an underlining fear in her patient's resentment, Dr. Holland first tried empathy, then reason. "I understand how devastating this accident has been for you and Ms. Gibson, but you are both fortunate that you have families who love you and want to take care of you."

"Avis loves my money, not me. If you can find my son Dakota, THEN I'll go home with family."

The young physician patted her patient's arm, "I wish you could stay here longer, Ms. Wayland, unfortunately, insurance and other circumstances dictate the length of your stay."

"Get that redheaded freak out of here," Emma interjected, "she's crazier than a werewolf with mange."

"Emma, mind your own business or I'll sedate you and call your sister," Dr. Holland replied.

"Don't you dare call Sister Mary Rose Catherine! That woman will put me in her convent until I'm dead," Emma warned.

"Okay then, be quiet while I'm talking to Ms. Wayland."

Dr. Holland gently laid her hand on Grandy's arm and asked in a barely audible voice, "Are you afraid for your safety if you stayed with Avis? Would he or anybody living in his house hurt you?"

"Hell no, I can take care of myself. He and his family just want to lock me away in some old fart's nursing home and spend all my money."

"Maybe you should contact a lawyer."

"My son is a lawyer, somebody needs to send him to another planet for deprogramming."

It was difficult to suppress a laugh but the kind doctor did so. It was imperative that she convince her eccentric patient that she had no other choice but to go back to Minnesota with her son.

* * * * *

It didn't take Bernice long to pack the few items she had in the hospital room. She tried to stretch out the task so that saying goodbye to Grandy would not become an actual event. The two friends had already discussed a possible future reunion and a promise to call each other often. Both of them knew though, how good intentions can get tossed into the busy crevices of life. The relationship between Bernice and Charlotte was evidence of that.

Bernice, once again, had small streams of tears on her face as she stood next to her traveling companion of the last few months.

"Goodbye Grandy, don't forgot to call me once in a while," Bernice sniffled.

"Wipe your nose, Bernie. I'll be to Texas before you know it to pick your broadening bottom up for another trip."

Bernice smiled and gave her friend a hug.

"Enough, Old Lady, Joyce is waiting for you."

Before Bernice rounded the corner of the doorway, she turned to Grandy and said, "Thanks for everything."

"Yeah, yeah, you're welcome." The redhead sounded tough. When she was sure Bernice was gone from sight, her throat knotted up with tears. Her rough interior was beginning to dissolve into the image of a compassionate human being.

* * * * *

The silence between mother and daughter was uncomfortable, but necessary. Bernice's heart danced with elation at the thought of holding her baby granddaughter. The same heart crumbled knowing her future was vague at best. Bernice took the aisle seat, looking out the small window at nothing in particular until she fell asleep.

Joyce watched as her mother slept, realizing how quickly she had aged in just a few short weeks. It was going to be a challenge having her mother, a new baby, a fourth marriage and recent move to a new state on her shoulders. If it wasn't for the strength and kindness of her handsome hubby Buck, Joyce would have easily been able to walk away from it all.

As the landing announcement and instructions were given, Bernice awoke from her short nap. She peered out the window as the plane approached the Midland-Odessa Airport. There were no mountains, no trees, just flat, dry plains as far as the eye could see.

"Here we are, Mom." Joyce stated. "You doing okay?"

"Yeah, I guess. What time is it?"

"It's 6:45 a.m. and I bet Jackie is waiting for you."

Bernice smiled expansively at the thought of her grandbaby. "Is Buck okay watching after her?"

"He's great. And he is rarely alone. His mother and his aunts can't get enough of either of them. They're going have both of them spoiled rotten."

"Kind of like your daddy did to you?"

"Yeah, I guess. Like you always said, turn about's fair play."

"I'm gonna need to do a little shopping sometime today. It'll probably be a while before my things get here from Idaho."

"That Bud and Flossy are sure nice people."

"Yes they are. If it wasn't for them, we'd probably still be dangling from our seatbelts."

"We'll get you settled and then I'll take you shopping. If you want, you can call Grandy later, to see how she's doing."

Bernice's eyes lit up. "That would be great! I sure hope her and Avis can mend the fence."

"Bigger miracles have happened, Mom."

"That's very true."

Chapter 42

Avis rented a small C size coach motor home to drive Grandy back to Minnesota. He wanted the bed for her to lie on and needed the additional space for her belongings and Ditch. Before the Wayland crew even left Bud and Flossie's driveway, both mother and son were on their cell phones. Avis was calling his wife Liza and Grandy was calling Dog Face.

"Hello."

"Hi Liza, it's me."

"Hey Honey, how's it going? Are you on your way home?"

"Yes, finally." Avis' voice sounded like a thin paper trail. "We should be to St. Paul sometime Thursday night."

"How much trouble did your mother give you?" There was hesitation in Liza's voice as she envisioned the disorder that would soon erupt at their home.

"No more than the usual. She has a broken leg so at least she can't chase me."

"I had Consuelo put some fresh flowers in the spare bedroom and I rented a wheelchair for Grandy to get around in."

"That's sweet of you Liza, thank you, but my mother has her own wheelchair, remember?"

"Oh that's right, I forgot." There was a pause before Liza continued, "I talked Augusta into preparing a little song and dance skit to perform for her grandma. She grumbled a bit about being too old for that stuff, but I told her that it would cheer Grandy up."

Knowing his wife all too well, Avis rolled his eyes and asked, "You didn't happen to promise her the latest high-tech gadget, did you?"

Silence from the other end of the phone line told Avis he was right, but because he was tired and anxious to get home, he didn't lecture Liza on child rearing protocol.

160

While Avis was busy chatting with his wife, Grandy was finally able to get a hold of Dog Face.

"Hello."

"Where the hell have you been, Dale Evans Krone!" There was no mistaking the rage in the redhead's voice.

"I've been - "

"I don't care where you've been, you should have dropped everything and come to my bedside the minute I called you," Grandy's anger was topped with sprinkles of being overwhelmed.

"I told you, Sis, I was waiting on parts for my truck. They just came this morning, give me a few hours to put them in and I can be on my way to get you late this afternoon."

"Too late, Bonehead, I'm in a cracker box motor home that Avis rented and he's driving me to his place as we speak. You need to be waiting outside his house when we get there to pick me up. I will not spend one night where even the Addam's Family would be afraid."

"Is Miss Bernice with you?"

"Never mind about Bernice, she doesn't like you anyway."

"That's mean, Sister."

"Yeah well, get over it. You need to make sure you are waiting outside Avis' place. We should be there sometime Thursday night. Don't make me spend more time than I have to with my oddball offspring."

"Now Grandy, you shouldn't talk about Avis like that, he's your son," Dog Face said.

"Are you siding with Avis? Cause if you are, Dog Face, I'll pull those droopy jowls of yours over the top of your head and tie them in a knot."

"Slow down Sis, you know I don't like my nephew that much. But I don't think you have to worry about him killing you for insurance money."

"You don't know what I have to worry about. See you tomorrow night." Grandy hung up the phone.

* * * * *

A few hours into Montana, Avis entered the parking lot of a log cabin style restaurant in Bozeman. He walked to the back of the motor home to see if his mother was ready for some supper.

"Mom," Avis said softly, "are you hungry?"

Grandy and Ditch opened their eyes at the same time. They blinked, stretched, and then sat up.

"Where are we?" Grandy asked.

"At a restaurant in Bozeman, Montana. I figured it was time to have something to eat. I'll get you into your wheelchair and we'll go inside for awhile."

"You need to take Ditch outside so he can pee," Grandy said with authority.

"That's fine. When we come back in, I'll get you into your wheelchair and we'll go inside for awhile."

"Does this place have entertainment?"

Avis glanced at his mother's red hair which had twisted itself into the shape of a small cyclone. Grandy was wearing one of her neon green, UFO shirts and her mascara had melted into dark half moon circles under her eyes.

"Don't worry about entertainment Mom, I'm sure we'll find something."

Chapter 43

"Mommy's home," Buck announced to his daughter who smiled from her baby seat. Buck opened the front door and gave his wife a hug. "You made it."

"Yeah, we made it. Can you get Mom's things?"

"No problem. Hi, Mom, good to see you." Buck kissed Bernice on the cheek and proceeded to the driveway.

"Hi, Buck."

Joyce picked up Jackie and turned to her mother. "I know you're dying to hold her. Have a seat over there."

"First I gotta pee."

Joyce directed her mother towards the bathroom and then held the front door open for Buck.

"Is she gonna be okay?"

"She'll be fine. Just a broken arm and a few bruises. More than anything, she's shook up over the whole ordeal."

"How's Grandy doing?"

"She broke her leg. I guess she's going to live with her son." Joyce then took her voice down to a whisper. "I'm just glad to get Mom away from that crazy woman."

"She is a character, but do you really think she's crazy?"

"She drove the motor home into a ditch because she saw Big Foot. If that's not crazy, I don't know what is."

"Your home is very nice," Bernice remarked as she returned to the livingroom.

"It's your home, now, too, Mom," Buck announced.

"You're sweet, Buck, we'll see. I'll try not to wear out my welcome." Bernice then sat down on the sofa and set a pillow over her cast. Joyce gently placed the baby in Grandma's arms.

"Oh, she's even more beautiful than I remember." Tears welled in Bernice's eyes as she softly stroked Jackie's forehead.

"She's gonna be your roommate for a couple of days, if that's okay." Joyce stated. "We're still unpacking boxes out of the spare bedroom, but we'll have it fixed up for you in no time."

"I don't mind at all sharing a room with this precious, little angel. Don't go to any trouble on my account."

"It's no trouble at all. It will get my butt in gear to finally finish unpacking."

* * * * *

Buck was more than willing to watch Jackie so Joyce could take her mother shopping. Bernice surveyed her surroundings and was struck by the dry, desolation and many miles between homes. A horse ranch separated Joyce and Buck's 900 square foot abode from a larger and much newer ranch-style house.

"That's where Buck's parents live." Joyce noted. "They own all this property, about 150 acres, including our house. And over there, that's his Aunt Ola and Uncle Sam. And that's Aunt Nettie and Uncle Dean's place." Joyce pointed to two other older homes, much the same style as Buck and Joyce's.

"The family owns the horse ranch, too?"

"All this land has been in their family for three generations. During the Depression it was all planted in cotton. Buck's grandfather actually sold off part of a larger piece of land and later on Buck's Dad had the big house built where the grandparents' house used to be. The house where we live is actually where Buck's parents lived when he was born."

"Where does Buck work?"

"He's not working right now. He's taking a little time off to regroup. Running the car lot was pretty stressful for him. He plans on maybe helping his brother-in-law at his mechanic's shop in town."

"Where's the town?"

"You'll see. There's only about five or six thousand people in Gunther, including the outlying areas, so it's probably smaller than what you're used to, living in Minneapolis."

"Or you either, living in Los Angeles."

"And I'm so glad to be out of there. This is a wonderful place to raise a child."

Bernice took it all in, wondering how long she would be able to live with no mountain ranges, no majestic redwoods, and no Grandy. She even missed Ditch.

"Maybe I can call Grandy when we get back from shopping."

"Sure, Mom. That's a great idea."

Chapter 44

The grilled steak dinner including fresh corn on the cob, BBQ beans, seasoned potatoes and homemade strawberry shortcake packed Avis' and Grandy's stomachs like piglets in a sow. They left the Bozeman restaurant, the son walking slowly as he pushed his mother's wheelchair to the motor home.

"I"m sorry Mom, but I don't think I can drive much longer tonight," Avis moaned as he helped Grandy back to the Fleetwood bed, "I'm so full I could just die."

The exhausted grandma decided not to reply to her son's comment, thinking the words would probably be misinterpreted.

"You need to take Ditch for a pee walk and feed him my leftover scraps," Grandy commanded.

"Let's find a campground outside of town, then I'll take him. I'm not going to do it in the restaurant parking lot."

"Why not, I do it all the time."

"Because, Mother, it's rude and inconsiderate."

"Fine. Just hurry up and find a campground, I need a sponge bath." Grandy repositioned her pillows, then began looking around for something to slide inside her cast in order to scratch her itchy leg.

Avis shook his head and said, "Maybe I'll go back inside and ask where we can set up for the night."

"Look in one of my boxes for my KOA Campground Directory, and while you're at it, see if you can find a ruler, spatula or wire coat hanger. My leg itches like a Minnesota Mosquito Fest." Grandy's tone of voice was clearly on an agitation setting.

"I'm going inside to ask. By the time I find the KOA directory, it'll be morning. As far as your leg itching, take one of the pills your doctor gave you for that; a coat hanger with only make the situation worse." Avis exited the motor home before his mother could add more insult to the mental wounds. He was unable to completely escape the words she shouted as he shut the door.

"Avis, don't' forget Ditch!"

* * * * *

It was nearly midnight before Avis could lay down on the pullout couch. If the driving, overeating and his mom's caustic remarks weren't enough of a full briefcase, then trying to figure out how to set up the motor home for water, sewer and power was even more challenging. Since he knew very little about the whole system, he depended on Grandy to yell instructions to him and describe the parts and connections that went together.

There was also Ditch to walk, feed and water. The mutt was eager for attention after being cooped up. Once again, Avis felt the invisible handgrip of his mother to obey her wishes, which was to play fetch with her dog in the dark.

* * * * *

There was little to see and little to talk about, as Avis and Grandy made their way across the rest of Montana and North Dakota. The barren bluffs, high deserts and prairies were a sad brown, summer already rushing to get out. Both mother and son had time to regurgitate their feelings for each other and what caused so much disunion between them. Because pride and stubbornness was a major part of their personalities, they knew "talking it out" would never happen.

Thursday afternoon, the pair crossed the Minnesota border. Grandy's demeanor softened a bit as she entered her home state. Almost immediately the site of farms, corn fields and tall, expansive trees filled her chest with a comforting familiarity. She sat at the motor home dinette, her leg propped up, dividing her attention between the scenery and her solitaire card game.

"We're almost home, Mom. Just a few more hours," Avis announced. It was one of many attempts to engage the feisty redhead into a civilized conversation.

"Don't talk to me, Son, I'm still madder than a mouse in a no exit maze. It's all your fault I'm on my way to a house filled with glass coffee tables and carrot juice enemas."

"What are you talking about? How is all this my fault?"

"If you hadn't been chasing after me, I wouldn't have gone off the side of the road."

"You crashed because you were hallucinating again about mythical creatures. And just to set the record right, we do not use carrot juice enemas at our house." Avis' voice was firm but not overly rough. He slid his fingers through his silver streaked hair. There were several moments of silence before Avis dared speak again, "Mom, are you going to be mad at me forever?"

"No, just until I put your lawyer butt in a blender."

* * * * *

A shell pink evening sky welcomed Avis as he pulled along the curb in front of his house. After a deep breath, he unbuckled his seatbelt and walked to the back of the Fleetwood. Grandy had laid down for a nap on the bed. The oldest son stared at his sleeping mother and began to really question whether he had made the right decision to bring her to his house. He glanced at the snoozing Ditch beside her and knew bringing the dog home was definitely not a good idea. Since both seemed dreaming of another planet, Avis left them alone and decided to go inside and prepare his family for the thunderstorm about to enter their lives.

Chapter 45

"Did you get a hold of Grandy?" asked Joyce.

"I left a message. Maybe she'll call me back tomorrow. Where's Buck?"

"Oh, he's over helping his mother do something. I don't know what she did before we moved out here. His dad's out on the ranch all day, and when he comes home, he's too tired to do anything around the house."

"How does Buck feel about that?"

"Oh, you know Buck. He'd do anything for anybody. That's what I love most about him, but his mom sees him now more than I do."

"Yoo-hoo! Anybody home?" A high-pitched voice echoed through the front door.

"Come on in, Nettie."

"Land's sakes it's hotter than blue blazes out there." An elderly woman, whose slender figure reminded Bernice of Grandy, entered the kitchen holding a peach pie."

"You're gonna have to stop doing that, Nettie. We're all gonna get fat around here."

"Nonsense, you skinny, little thang." The woman turned to Bernice. "Mercy, where's my manners. This must be your mama."

"Nice meeting you," Bernice extended her hand.

Nettie shooed away Bernice's hand and instead gave her a big hug. "We're all family here. Now where's Little Sugar."

"Jackie's sleeping, but she should be waking up any time."

"You have got the most precious little granddaughter. Do you have any other grandbabies?"

"No, Joyce is my only child."

"Well, Little Sugar is just precious, yes she is. I could just eat her up."

Bernice watched as Buck's aunt took over the kitchen, cleaning counters, washing dishes and talking the whole time.

Bernice then gave Joyce an inquisitive look. Joyce smiled and shrugged her shoulders as the woman pulled down three small plates from the cupboard and began cutting into her fresh pie.

"Oh, no, none for me, thanks," Bernice said politely.

"Come on, now, don't insult me. I made it especially for y'all."

Bernice could see Nettie was a bit put out so she agreed, "Just a little piece. It looks delicious."

As the three enjoyed their afternoon treat, another "yoo-hoo" came from the front door.

"Come on in, Ola. We're in the kitchen."

Ola bore no likeness to her sister, Nettie. Her broad bottom dwarfed Bernice's, as she bounced into the room holding a cherry cobbler, fresh from the oven. "Save room for some of this, y'all."

"Oh, Ola, you shouldn't have," Joyce made room on the table for the hot dish.

"Is this your mama? Oh, my, your daughter is about the best thing that happened to our Buck. And that little princess, she's just the sweetest thang."

"Nice to meet you," again Bernice extended her hand and received another Texas style hug. Ola hugged Joyce and joined the ladies at the table.

The sisters queried Bernice on her travels. "Yeah, we heard y'all on the radio. That Grandy sounds like a hoot," Nettie stated.

"Oh, she's quite a character, alright," Bernice agreed. "This pie is delicious but I can't eat another bite."

"Why not? Is there something wrong?"

"She'd rather have some of my cobbler," Ola interjected. "Here, I'll cut you a piece."

"Oh, no, no. Really. I'm fine. It's all wonderful. I'm just full, that's all."

"My peach pie won first prize at the fair last summer."

"Well my cobbler recipe was featured in the Gunther News."

"Yeah, just because your daughter works at the newspaper."

"That's not the only reason."

"Is too."

The bantering sisters reminded Bernice of her travels with Grandy. Bernice and Joyce silently watched the entertainment while smiling at each other.

"Y'all are coming to our house for Sunday supper, right?"

"I don't know, Nettie. I'll have to check with Buck."

"But I'm cooking Sunday supper," Ola interrupted.

Jackie's crying broke up the conversation. Joyce left the room. The friendly arguing changed gears to who was going to hold the baby first and who the baby liked best. Bernice could only imagine how this sibling rivalry must have driven Buck's grandmother crazy when they were growing up, and thanked her lucky stars she had only had one child.

Joyce brought Jackie into the kitchen and grabbed her bottle from the warmer. The grandma and the two aunts followed her into the livingroom, ooing and awing at the little bundle. Joyce then placed Jackie into her mother's lap. Bernice was able to hold the bottle in her broken arm. She kissed the sweet smelling top of her granddaughter's head. She smiled at her granddaughter, knowing that, of the three older women, she, Bernice Gibson, was most important in this precious, little girl's life.

Chapter 46

A loud buzzing noise circled Grandy's head and her long boney arm instinctively reached out and swiped at it. The lightweight mosquito was no match for the old woman's 60+ years of expertise in insect destruction, and it instantly fell apart in midair. Still groggy from her nap, Grandy slowly opened her eyes and shrieked as an oddly dressed figure stared at her from the end of the bed.

"Hi Grandma," said an adolescent voice, its pitch a mixture of curiosity and caution, "Dad said I should come out here and check on you."

"Who are you?" Grandy growled.

"I'm Augusta."

As Grandy studied her granddaughter, Ditch began barking at the stranger before him.

"That's an ugly dog," Augusta said as she crunched her face.

"You're no trophy yourself. That hair of yours looks like blue barf and your clothes remind me of something Bernice would wear."

"I'm gonna tell my parents you said that."

Grandy scooted herself closer to the end of the bed and looked Augusta directly in the eye, "Do I look like I care?"

The young girl stared back at her grandma and as she turned to leave said, "You'd better be nice to me, 'cause Dad's talking to mom about checking you into a psych hospital."

* * * * *

It was only a few moments later when Avis showed up to help his mother into the house. He had instructed Augusta to walk Ditch and gave her a small shovel and plastic baggie to pick up the dog's poop.

"But Dad! That's so gross! Besides, that stupid mutt barks at me, he'll probably bite me, too."

Avis looked at Grandy in frustration and said, "Well, I can't do everything. Is Augusta going to have a problem with your dog?"

Ditch's owner reached down and petted him on the head. "It's alright Baby, the brat can take you out to tinkle. No barking or biting unless absolutely necessary." Grandy handed the leash to Augusta and said, "He'll be fine. Just don't yank on the leash or walk him past yards that have those bright colored knomes, he hates those things."

Augusta reluctantly left with Ditch while Avis helped his mother into her wheelchair and pushed her into the house. Liza was standing in the foyer, her arms out stretched ready to hug Grandy.

"Welcome to our home, Mom, it's good to see you!" The middle-aged woman started towards her mother-in-law when Grandy held up a hand.

"Stop right there Lulu, I already know you and Mr. Greedy here are planning to ship me off to a mental hospital. I'll have you know that even with this cast on, I can create quite a ruckus and – "

"Mom," Avis touched her shoulder, "*Liza* and I are not planning on sending you to a psych ward. We just wanted a safe place for you to recuperate." Isn't that right, Honey?" Avis' green eyes pleaded with his wife for solidarity.

"That's not what Augusta said, she – hey, wait a minute, I said mental hospital and you said psych ward. Ha! I knew you were scheming to get rid of me."

Avis' voice moved from a cooperating mode to miffed. "Alright, that's enough Mother, it's been a long trip, I'm tired and I don't need anymore of your paranoia. I'm wheeling you into the spare bedroom and LIZA will be in to assist you with whatever else you need tonight."

Avis breezed past the two women and upstairs to his bedroom. Liza smiled timidly at Grandy and said with a false airiness, "Okay then, let's check out your room. You have your own private bath, T.V. and a very comfortable bed. When you get tired of T.V., you can people watch out the big bay window from your room. I'll even bring some warm milk and homemade cookies once you've settled in."

The annoyed senior citizen closed her eyes and attempted a civil tongue, "Thank you Liza, a little help to clean up for the night would be great, but please no milk and cookies. My system is long over due for a glass of vino and a large bag of Cheetos."

* * * * *

Later that night, when the Wayland family had gone to bed, Grandy peered out her bay window for the hundredth time. She was silently fuming inside that Dog Face had not been waiting for her like she had instructed. Grandy pulled her cell phone out of her pocket and dialed her brother's number.

"Yeah."

"Where the hell are you?" Grandy seethed, "you were supposed to be here hours ago to pick me up."

"Who is this?"

"It's me, your sister, you moron. Why aren't you here?"

There was no way to misinterpret the anger in Old Red's voice.

"Um, I sorta had a problem with my pickup, Sis. It's going to be out of commission for awhile."

"Now what happened? I thought all you had to do was put the parts in your truck and you'd be on your way." Grandy's free hand twirled strands of her red hair into small knots.

"I'll tell you what happened, Grandy, but you have to promise not to yell at me" Bottom line fear was in Dog Face's voice.

174

"Brother, you'll have a lot more to worry about besides my screaming if the reason you aren't here is a dim-witted one."

Silence wormed its way through the phone line between siblings.

"Dog Face, you still there?"

"Yeah Grandy, I'm still here. Okay, here it goes. After I got my pickup all fixed up, I decided to test it out by going out by Old Exley's Pond. You know, how that gravel road around it is just perfect checking out steering and braking capacities. Well, just as I was into the most awesome turn, I spit out the window the last small piece of snuff in my mouth. The wind whipped it back into the pickup and right into my eye. I was so surprised that I took both hands off the steering wheel to wipe it away and that's when the pickup decided to keep turning a tight left circle, right into the pond." Dog Face took a deep breath before continuing, "I'm sorry Grandy, it was an accident. Grandy? You still there? Grandy?"

Chapter 47

Grandy's new surroundings and fuming anger at her brother kept her awake most of the night. Shortly after she finally fell asleep, Ditch licked her face. At Avis' instructions, Augusta had shut the bedroom door so the mutt could not leave any surprises in other rooms of the house.

"If you people don't want Ditch peein' on your carpet, you better come and get him right now!" Grandy hollered.

Avis was the only one up and hurried to his mother's room before she woke everyone else. "How are you feeling, Ma?"

"How do you think I feel? You could have at least given up your bedroom, with the big, comfy bed. Was this Augusta's bed when she was 5 or what? Get me up in the wheelchair and then take Ditch out to pee."

"No problem, Ma. Liza will be up soon and fix you some breakfast."

"Swell."

After Avis exited the room, Grandy dug through her handbag for Joyce's phone number. Before turning on her cell phone, she noticed there was a telephone on the night stand next to the bed.

"I'll show old Money Bags. I'll run up his phone bill." Grandy dialed Joyce's number.

"Hello."

"Grandy here. Let me talk to your mother."

"Sure, Grandy. I'll see if she's up."

Bernice had heard the phone and immediately exited the room, assuming it was Grandy. Not wanting to wake Jackie, she closed the door behind her."

"Is it Grandy?"

"Yeah, you wanna take it in the kitchen?"

"Sure.... Hello."

"We gotta get a plan. I'm goin' nuts over here."

"What's wrong?"

"Well, for starters, these people are weird. My granddaughter thinks she's a rock star, my son thinks he's my father and his wife thinks she can cook. They've got me in a munchkin bed that's hard as a rock, my leg itches and I've got claustrophobia. Oh, and did I mention, they want to take me to the psych ward?"

"Oh, Grandy, I don't believe that."

"Oh, yeah? Avis already made an appointment with a doctor. He said it's for my leg, but I know better."

"Maybe it is for your leg. Don't you think you should have it checked out?"

"I don't need it checked out. When my six weeks are up, I'm sawing this thing off and that'll be the end of it."

"I hope you're right, Grandy. Aren't you gonna ask how I'm doin'?"

"Let me guess. They put you in with the baby, who wakes you up every two hours, your clothes are starting to smell like spit-up, and it's hot and dry. I've had babies and I've been to Texas."

"You left out Buck's family."

"What about 'em?"

"Oh, they're all nice and all. There's just so many of them. He's got two aunts who live right down the road, his parents lives next door, and there are cousins and nieces and nephews too numerous to count and they are in and out of the house all day long. His two aunts are fighting over whose doing Sunday supper. Oh, but his Aunt Nettie reminds me of you, Grandy."

"How come? Does she like UFO's?"

"No, she's just kinda looks like you."

"Does she have red hair?"

"No."

"Does she have blue eyes?"

"No."

"Does she have a broken leg or sit in a wheelchair?"

"No."

"Then how the hell does she remind you of me?"

"She's skinny like you are."

"Are you sure the doctor didn't give you a hallucinogenic drug, Bernie? I think your normal meter is off a few numbers."

"Never mind, Grandy."

"We need to talk about our plan. Dog Face owes me big time. He stood me up, twice."

"Oh, do we have to involve him?"

"Yes, we have to involve him," Grandy answered in a mocking tone. "Who else are we gonna get?"

"Maybe Buck."

"What's Buck gonna do? The motor home is in Iowa, he's in Texas, with a wife and kid. No, Bernie, it's gotta be Dog Face."

Bernice became nauseous just hearing his name. She racked her brain for another alternative. "What about Bud?"

"Bud can't even go pee without Flossy's permission."

"Well, I think she'd give him permission to help us out."

"Yeah, but then we have to deal with her, too."

"I like Flossy."

"Her hair is too black."

Bernice was about to ask what that had to do with anything, but decided it wasn't worth the detour in conversation.

"The way I figure it, soon as I can put full weight on my leg, I'll be fine. In the meantime, I'll get Dog Face to go to Iowa and fix the motor home."

"But they said it was totaled."

"Well, they've never met my brother."

"You do what you gotta do, Grandy. Give me a call sometime." If the only way to see Grandy again was to be in the presence of Dog Face, Bernice had a tough choice to make.

"Don't be so negative, Bernie. You know you wanna get back out on the road as much as I do."

"Well, yeah, but let's be realistic."

"Realistic! What we've done in the past few months has gone beyond realistic. Think about it. What if we hadn't taken dirt roads and detours. We'd still be counting ceiling tiles and playing Bingo with the likes of Leisure Suit Larry."

"You're right. Call me when you find out something."

"You just get ready. It can't be too much longer, or I'll be checking myself into the psych ward."

The ladies both laughed and said their goodbyes.

Chapter 48

"Betty Stanley from Atlanta, come on down." *The Price is Right* just wasn't the same without Bob, Bernice thought. She focused her attention out the livingroom window at the dry, coarse landscape outside. Different scenarios of her future played in her head. Would she be stuck in this desolate land for the rest of her life? Would she just go to sleep and not wake up? Was Grandy serious about going back out on the road?

Cries from her granddaughter snapped Bernice into the present. She turned off the television and went into the kitchen where Joyce was preparing a bottle for Jackie.

"I was wondering -" Bernice's question was cut short by a shrill greeting coming through the door.

"Yoo-hoo!"

"And here's another one. Come on in, Mother."

Yet another gray-haired grandma entered the kitchen, this one holding a three-layer chocolate cake. She was an average-sized woman, but much shorter than Ola and Nettie.

"Mom, I'd like you to meet Grace Arbuckle, Buck's mom. Mother, this is my mom, Bernice Gibson."

Bernice and Grace shook hands and exchanged pleasantries, as Joyce set the cake on the counter.

Grace then picked up the baby. "There, there. It's okay. Grammy's here."

A streak of jealousy struck in the pit of Bernice's stomach. She couldn't compete with the grandmother who lived right next door, not to mention her broken arm that made it difficult to pick up her own granddaughter. Joyce handed Grace the bottle and they all sat down in the kitchen.

"Isn't our granddaughter just the prettiest little thang?" the Texas grandma cooed as she stroked Jackie's baby fine hair.

"Yes, she certainly is," Bernice agreed.

"Buck shooed me out of the kitchen so he could work on my sink, it's backed up again. Land's sakes, I just don't know what I'd do without him."

Joyce wanted to ask, "what DID you do without him," or "what are you going to do when he gets a real job?" but she didn't know her mother-in-law well enough to dish out such tart questions.

"So you already met Nettie and Ola?"

"Yes, they were here yesterday. They're so much taller than you are."

"Oh, Dear, Nettie and Ola are Buck's daddy's sisters. I have three sisters and four brothers, but they all live in the Dallas area."

"That explains it."

"Joyce told me about your radio show. That's interesting."

"Yeah, it was kind of exciting. Did you ever hear the show."

"No, Dear, I don't have time to listen to the radio, or watch TV for that matter." Grace put the bottle down and put Jackie to her shoulder to burp her."

Bernice looked at her daughter and said, "That reminds me, Joyce. Do you think it would be alright if I used your phone to call Chet? He was nice enough to come see us at the hospital, I should let him know how I'm doing."

"Of course Mom, you don't even need to ask. Do you have the number?"

"No, I am hoping I can call information."

"Let me go on the Internet. I'll find it for you." Joyce went into the other room where the computer was set up and left the two grandmothers alone with their granddaughter.

"Joyce is a real sweet gal. You should be very proud."

"Oh, yes, I am. Buck is nice, too." Bernice tried to be cordial while watching the woman interact with her little granddaughter.

181

"Oh, do you want to hold her?"

"No, that's okay. It's kinda hard for me," Bernice raised her casted arm.

"Here's the number, Mom. You can go into the other room if you want some privacy."

"Thanks, Honey." Bernice went into the livingroom and dialed Chet's number.

"K-Taz Radio, may I help you?"

"Yes, I'd like to speak to Chet Baxter."

"He's on the air right now. Can I take a message?"

"Well, I was kind of hoping you could put me through. This is Bernice Gibson, you know, one of the traveling grandmas."

"Oh, yes, Ms. Gibson. How are you?" The receptionist's voice was one of genuine concern.

"Doing very well, thanks for asking. Would you be able to put me through?"

"No problem. I'm sure he'd be happy to take your call."

After a short pause, Chet came on the line. "Bernice, how are you? We've just been talking about you and Grandy."

"I'm doing alright. Are we on the air right now?"

"No, it's a commercial break and my assistant will take over if we're still talking. Where are you?"

"I'm down in Texas visiting my daughter and her family."

"How's your arm?"

"Oh, it's fine, just a little itchy. It's really hot down here."

"How is Grandy? Is she with you?"

"Oh, no, she's staying with her son's in St. Paul. I talked to her last night. She seems to be doing okay. Kinda antsy, though. You know Grandy."

"I'll bet. This isn't the son – "

"Sure is. I'm pretty shocked myself, that she let him talk her into going with him. I don't think she had much of a choice, though."

182

"Well, I'm so glad you called, Bernice. I didn't have any way of getting a hold of you to tell you that your sister, Char called the show yesterday. She heard about the accident on the radio and is very worried about you."

"Did she leave you a number? I had it, but now I can't find it. I think it's still in the motor home."

"I sure do. If you stay on the line, I'll get you that number right away. I'm so glad you called. You have no idea how many fans you have. Since the accident, the phone lines have been lit up like New York City at night. Hope you get out on the road again, soon. We all miss you."

"I miss you, too. Thanks, Chet." Bernice choked back the tears. She stayed on the line and then thanked Chet for sister's phone number.

* * * * *

"Joyce, I'm going to call Charlotte."

"Sounds good, tell her hello for me."

Bernice dialed the number and received a recording from Henry's phone. She left a message, assuring Charlotte that she was fine and gave her Joyce's phone number.

At supper time, Char returned a call to her sister. The two chatted for an hour while Bernice's meatloaf meal became cold. It was determined that Christmas would be celebrated together and on New Year's Day, they would visit their old redheaded friend in Minnesota.

Chapter 49

The weeks had been slowly rolling past Grandy like a heavy March fart. Avis and Liza did their best to make their consistently crabby family member comfortable. At Grandy's insistence, Liza used her expertise in cosmetology to re-dye her mother-in-law's hair to a shade of red resembling a ripe tomato. Avis avoided any conversation concerning money and Augusta decided Ditch wasn't so bad and started teaching him tricks. To the outside world, the household seemed to be forming an amicable unit. No one suspected that during the midnight hours, Grandy was using her laptop to express her restlessness in the ISAET (I Saw An Extraterrestrial) chat room.

* * * * *

An early morning argument between Howard and Blackie was interrupted by the telephone.

"What!" Howard shouted into the receiver.

"Whoa Brother, I'm not the dog who bit you."

Howard took a deep breath then continued, "Sorry Dakota, I was in the middle of a discussion with Blackie."

"Was it a discussion or a fight?"

"Okay, a fight. She's ready to walk if Dad doesn't leave in the next couple of days."

There was surprise and a bit of disappointment in Dakota's voice as he said, "I didn't know Dad was living with you."

"Yeah well, he just showed up unannounced and made himself at home."

"Let me guess, it didn't take Blackie long to tire of his farting, belching and gross hygiene?" Dakota said dryly.

"You're right. Blackie is used to the less than clean habits of her brother Z, but Dad goes beyond the border with her. Yesterday the old man left his toenail clippings on the kitchen table and used her toothbrush because he had dropped his in the toilet."

"I'm sure Dad gets some sort of retirement benefits from either the government or his former place of employment. Drive him to another city or state and help him find a cheap place to live."

"You suggestion sounds good, why don't you come help me with it?" Howard's voice sounded worn down. Dakota could visualize his younger brother's pale blue eyes closed, his blue collar hand shoved in his jeans pocket in frustration.

"Where is Dad now?"

"I gave him a twenty to get him out of the house. I'm sure he's gone to the local pub."

"A twenty doesn't cover many drinks these days."

Howard exhaled, "I know, but the bartender is a friend of mine and he'll stretch it out so Dad should be gone at least an hour."

"Does he know about the accident and where Mom is?"

"Unfortunately yes to both questions. He heard about the accident from the Chet Baxter show and immediately called Avis. Our attorney sibling told him Mom was staying with him. He did have the decency to tell Lester to stay away though, as there wasn't any motor home to go after."

Dakota sounded almost jubilant as he said, "there should be no reason for our father to bother Mom anymore. The only thing he really wanted was half the proceeds from her Fleetwood."

There was a pause before Howard replied, "I wish that were the case. Dad seems to think she still has a bunch of money somewhere since she was able to afford to travel the country. I tried to explain to him that the expenses of her trips were shared with her friend Bernice. He still believes she's hiding something. I hear him muttering to himself about 'borrowing' a vehicle or getting a bus ticket to go visit her at Avis'."

"Well Howard, how are we going to stop that?" Dakota's tone of voice was controlled but its roots were boiling with anger and Howard could sense it.

"I think I have an idea Brother," said the beer truck driving man with a smile on his face.

Dakota and Howard talked about the formula to disable Lester's plans to see their mother. Part of it involved the two of them going to Avis' the next week to see Grandy. They figured out the day, time and where to meet first. Before hanging up, the brothers bragged about their respective families and laughed over a couple of childhood memories. Dakota explained his determination to pursue the unknown riches of a treasure map. The phone call ended with Dakota convinced his younger brother may have shifted his neutrality to a firm supportive role of their mother.

Chapter 50

The next two months seemed an eternity for Bernice. Having the cast removed from her arm did little to settle her anxieties about her future. Her days in Texas were long and uneventful. She was happy to spend time with Joyce and her family, but felt out of place. Buck's relatives were nice, but she had nothing in common with them, except an adoration for little Jackie. Their daily visits brought so many calories that she could already hear Grandy telling her how big her butt was getting. After careful consideration, Bernice made a decision which would, hopefully, help decide her fate.

"Joyce, can I talk to you?"

"Sure, Mom, what's up?"

"I really appreciate you letting me stay with you."

"Don't be silly, Mom, our home is your home."

"I know. You and Buck are so sweet, but I think I need to get away for a few days."

"What do you mean?"

"I was thinking about flying up to Minnesota to visit some old friends."

Joyce was only a smidgen surprised. She had sensed her mother's restlessness shortly after Bernice had arrived in Texas. It didn't take Bernice mentioning Grandy everyday for Joyce to know that is who her mother missed.

"Sure, Mom, whatever you want to do. I'd offer to go with you, but I think it would be too difficult with Jackie."

"Don't worry, I'll be fine." Bernice tried to make the visit look like only that, a short visit. She didn't have the heart to tell her daughter that she hated Texas and was considering moving back to Minnesota.

"When would you like to go?"

"Oh, anytime. Do you have a travel agent?"

"I'll handle it for you, Mom. Where will you stay?"

"If I can't stay with my friend, I'll get a hotel. Don't worry."

"This friend wouldn't happen to be Grandy, would it?"

"Heavens, no. She's still at Avis'. I don't want any part of that drama."

Joyce laughed. "You're probably right. How long will you be staying?"

"I'm not really sure. I'll just get a one-way ticket for now."

Joyce called the airline the next day and was able to get her mother on an early morning flight two days later.

* * * * *

"Do you have everything?" Joyce picked up Bernice's suitcase.

"I think so. I need to kiss my granddaughter goodbye and then I'll be ready to go."

"She's in the kitchen with her daddy."

As much as she disliked living in Texas, Bernice knew she would miss her granddaughter terribly. Tears welled up in Bernice's eyes as she held Jackie close and kissed her soft forehead. She handed Jackie back to Buck, gave him a big hug and quickly went out to the car so no one would see her cry.

"I'll be there in a sec," Joyce announced. She then turned to Buck and whispered, "I'm really worried about Mom. Do you think I'm doing the right thing by letter her do this?"

"Joyce, she's a grown woman. I know she's very emotional right now, but think about what she's been through over the past few months. It'll be good for her to get away."

Buck always seemed to know exactly what to say. Joyce gave him a hug and kissed Jackie. "I'll be back in a couple of hours."

Few words were spoken between mother and daughter on the trip to the airport. Bernice watched the bland, barren scenery pass her by. She looked forward to autumn in the Cities, the cool breeze on her face and the bright red, orange and yellow hues from the tree-lined streets.

Joyce unloaded Bernice's things and walked her to her gate. "Are you gonna be okay, Mom?"

"I'll be fine, Dear. You take care my granddaughter."

"I will. And you be sure and call me as soon as you land."

"I will. I love you."

"I love you, too."

Chapter 51

A brilliant multi-colored fall welcomed a tired Bernice to Minnesota. She knew she should have called Grandy during her layover in Denver, but decided her arrival in Minneapolis would be too late for anyone to pick her up. She decided to stay the night in a hotel and call her friend the next morning.

Bernice stood on the curb with her suitcase and waved her flabby white arm to flag down a cab. The green and white taxi whipped in next to the curb and the driver jumped out. When Bernice and the cab driver's eyes met, they immediately recognized each other. Habib muttered, "Oh no, not this woman again," and he turned to get back into his cab to leave. Memories were still fresh as he recalled that, just a few short months ago, he had the misfortune of being the driver, twice, who chauffeured Bernice and her friend to various places. The one standing on the curb was also a lousy tipper, and she had paid him in nickels and dimes. He also remembered a stop at a liquor store on the way to the airport which nearly got him fired.

"Hey, where you going?" Bernice said in anger.

"You and your friend, bad luck for me," said Habib. His dark eyes darted around looking for the redheaded loose cannon.

"My friend isn't with me and I need a cab to the hotel. Just take me to the Marriott by the mall." Bernice knew this was one of the biggest hotels and, since it was the middle of the week, they would probably have a vacancy.

"Yes, Ma'am." Habib continued to murmur to himself as he drove to the hotel. "Surely Allah is upset with me. I must never again eat a hot dog with pork remains in it."

Bernice checked into the Marriott and immediately called Joyce to let her know she landed safely. "I got in kinda late, so I'm staying the night at the Marriott. I'll be seeing my friend tomorrow."

"Call me when you know where you'll be staying."

"I will. I love you."

"I love you, too, Mom. You be careful."

"Don't worry. I'll be fine. Bye-bye now."

"Bye."

Bernice took a shower and then ordered room service so she could take her pills. After eating half a tuna sandwich, she tried to go to sleep. The thought of seeing Grandy the next day kept her agitated enough that she ended up watching television until 3 a.m. before finally dozing off.

* * * * *

Grandy was not answering her cell phone, so Bernice dialed Avis' home phone number.

"Wayland residence."

"Yes, could I please speak with Grandy?"

"May I say who is calling?"

"This is Bernice."

"One moment please."

Grandy was right. Avis was a "hoity toity." He even had a maid answering the phone.

"I hope you're calling with a plan, Old Woman." Grandy said without even a hello to her former roommate.

"Hi Grandy. I'm here in Minnesota."

"What?"

"I'm here in Minnesota."

"What are you doing in Minnesota? Too many pablum stains on your clothes?"

"No, it just got too hot. I thought you'd want to get together and maybe go visit some old friends over at Passages."

"Darn right they're old, but they're not my friends. Why would I wanna go back there? Why would YOU wanna go back there?"

"I was thinking about maybe moving back in there. I just feel like I have no place to call my own. I hate Texas. I just want to be settled somewhere."

"What's wrong with living with your daughter and family? Do you whine more than the baby?"

Bernice could hear Grandy's muffled snicker. "NO! It's just a bit cramped with all of us in their house and my nerves are wearing thin with all Buck's side of the family constantly coming through the door."

"Why don't you rent a place of your own?"

"I told you, I don't like the bleakness of Texas. I miss the beautiful four seasons of Minnesota and - " Bernice hesitated, "and I miss you Grandy."

There was a long strip of silence before Grandy spoke, "well, we'll be back on the road soon."

"And how are we going to do that?"

"I told you Dale is gonna fix the motor home."

"Has he?"

"Well, no. He's been waiting for me to be able to travel with him."

"Do you still have the cast on your leg?"

"Yeah, but I'm about ready to saw it off here any day now, and we can be on our way."

"Well, I'd sure like to see you, Grandy. Are you allowed to leave Avis' house? He doesn't have some kind of device around your ankle that sounds an alarm if you leave, does he? I thought it would be fun if you'd go with me to Passages."

"No one puts anything on my ankle, especially Avis. I'll go when and where I please."

"Then why haven't you left yet?"

"I am, as soon as this doggone cast is off my leg."

"Will you please go to Passages with me, I'd really appreciate it," Bernice said in a soft plead.

"Fine Bernie, I'll go with you, just so I can talk you out of staying. I can't believe you'd really consider being in the same county as Leisure Suit Larry, let alone the same building."

"What other choices do I have, Grandy?" Bernice said in a weepy voice.

"Get a hold of yourself, Woman. Where are you right now? I'll pick you up and we'll go up to the home, if that's what you want to do."

"Thanks Grandy, I'll be waiting for you outside the Marriott next to the mall downtown. By the way, you'll never guess who my cabbie was last night?"

"Not Habib."

"Yes, Habib. He didn't seem too happy to see me."

"Gee, I wonder why?" The two mused as they recalled the adventure they afforded Habib on their trip to the airport.

"I'll be there in one hour, make sure you're ready to go. Hang up right now so you have enough time for your six layers of makeup and new coat of nail polish."

"Okay." Bernice hung up and for the first time since she'd met Grandy, she didn't mind the crazy broad's condescending remarks.

Chapter 52

Bernice readied her face for the trip to her former retirement home. Her normally coifed hair was in need of a rinse and cut but, since she had no time for either, the grey-haired grandma used a few bobby pins to keep the stray strands away from her face. Her salvation from a total meltdown was the fresh coat of Summer Apple Red nail polish. Bernice still felt unsettled with her uncertain future so, when she noticed she had forgotten to pack the matching lipstick to the nail polish, she sat down and balled.

"Get a hold of yourself." Was the voice beating around in the sad senior citizen's head. "That is exactly what Grandy would say," Bernice whimpered. So she gathered her faculties and took one more trip to the mirror to powder the red blotches her crying had produced.

Standing outside the door of the hotel, Bernice watched and waited for Grandy's arrival. Her heartbeat accelerated with the anticipation of seeing her old friend. As much as the two women had volleyed back and forth about every little thing, Bernice missed the low scoreboard redhead who had given her more excitement in just a few months than she had experienced in her entire 72 years.

"Oh, no. She wouldn't." Bernice recognized the choking sounds of the engine before the rusty green pickup came into view. The battered vehicle stopped abruptly in front of the waiting passenger. Inside, a clearly irritated redhead hit the driver with a large handbag.

"Miss Bernice, you are just as pretty as ever." Dale's large belly jiggled as he jumped out of the truck to greet her. His slovenly appearance hadn't changed since the last time Bernice had seen him. If anything, he was fatter, greasier and uglier than she remembered.

Grandy rolled down the passenger side window and hollered, "Hey Bernie, looks like they fed ya good down there in Texas."

A wide-eyed, paralyzed Bernice nodded her head in agreement and stared as Dog Face quickly approached her. Grandy's brother grabbed her blue-veined hand and gave it a cursory brown tobacco slobber kiss. Bernice pulled her hand from Dale's and immediately removed a moist towelette from her purse and to wipe her hand. She walked over to his pickup and tossed the towelette into the bed of the truck. Grandy was grinning at her friend as she said insistently, "Come on Bernie, get in the truck."

"My sister still has the cast on, so you can get in over here." Dale opened the driver's side door.

Bernice pursed her lips with a weak "thanks, then turned to her friend. "Hi Grandy, how are you doing?"

"I'd be a lot better if my lazy brother here would fix my motor home."

"If I told you once Grandy, I've told you a thousand times; Bud said the Fleetwood is destroyed, caput, died and gone to heaven. You'll just have to start saving your money for a new one," Dog Face said adamantly.

Grandy reached over Bernice and punched her brother in the arm.

"Ouch! What'd you do that for?"

"For not fixing my motor home and being so damn homely."

Dog Face let out a fart then changed the subject. "Where to, Ladies?"

"Bernie wants to go back to the home. God only knows why."

"Just for a visit. Aren't you even a little curious?"

"Curious about what? Nothing ever changes there."

"Well, we've been gone a long time."

"Bernie, in the four years you lived there, did anything every change?"

"Well, no."

"Then what makes you think, just because you've been gone for four months that something earthshaking has happened? And besides, who cares?"

"I care. Lillian was nice enough to call us when we were on the road."

"Yeah, when my son was trying to have me committed. That's another thing that never changes."

"How can you be sure he's trying to have you committed?"

"Just believe me. He is. And now you're here so we can put our heads together and come up with a plan to outsmart his twisted mind."

"I'll help," Dale interjected.

"Just drive, Dale. You already know how you fit into the plan. First thing you're gonna do is saw this cast off my leg."

"Don't you think you ought to have a doctor do that?" asked Bernice.

"No, because Dale will do it for free."

"What if it's not healed?"

"I'm fine."

The drive to the home seemed like an eternity as Bernice tried not to breathe too deeply. She was becoming nauseous from the onion and garlic aroma emanating from Dale's body and breath.

"Here we are." Dale pulled into *Passage of Time Retirement Home.*

"Get my chair, Dog."

"I thought you said you didn't want to go in," Dale exclaimed.

"Just get my chair and mind your own business."

"Yes, Ma'am." Dale gave his sister a sarcastic salute and removed her wheelchair from the back of the truck.

"I'll just sit out here and wait for ya. And Miss Bernice, if you need anything, anything at all, I'm here for ya."

"Thanks, I'll be fine." Bernice kept her distance from Dale as she exited the truck.

"Let's get this over with," Grandy said gruffly.

Chapter 53

Grandy was right. Nothing had changed, especially not the tan, black and faux gold wallpaper and the blaring television in the lobby. Two crippled, old women sat in their worn wheelchairs in front of the television, both sound asleep. Rounding the corner, Grandy and Bernice startled Loretta who was just coming out of the cafeteria.

"Bernice? Grandy? Is that you?"

"Hey, Loretta. How's it goin'?" Bernice asked.

"Want a candy bar I won at Bingo?"

"No thanks. Is Lillian working today?"

"Yeah, she's around here somewhere. Hey, did you hear about Nick and Ed?"

"No, what happened?"

"Dead. Both of them."

"What happened?" Bernice looked at Grandy with controlled hyperventilation. She wondered if the incident in the motor home before they left on the road was to blame. Grandy discreetly elbowed her friend as Loretta was yammering on about how the two guys died because of some severely spoiled wine one of the relatives had smuggled in.

"Oh, and did you hear about Larry and Trudy?" Loretta asked without missing a step.

"Them, too? Must be the food," Grandy surmised.

"Oh, no, it's nothing like that. They got married."

"To each other?" Grandy was dumbfounded.

"No way!" exclaimed Bernice.

"Yep, about a month ago. They're sharing a room now."

"Oh, I get it. Larry the tight wad." Grandy was certain it had to do with money. Trudy just didn't seem to be his type. She was built like a toothpick and kind of a ditz.

"No, I think they really love each other."

198

"Only thing Larry loves is Larry. Trudy was never very bright, but..."

"Shh, Grandy, here they come." Bernice interrupted.

Arm in arm, Larry, in his lime green leisure suit and rose-colored glasses, and paper thin Trudy, in her floral house dress, carrying her large, patent leather purse pranced down the hall.

"Well, well, well. I guess I win the bet," Larry announced loudly when he noticed Old Red sitting in her wheelchair.

"I don't think so, Pickle Face. We're just here for a visit with the real people."

"Nobody 'just visits.' I knew you'd be back. And you finally found a reason to be in the wheelchair. What'd ya do to your leg?"

"None of your business," Grandy snapped.

"We had -," Bernice started to explain.

"Shut up Bernie, it's nothin' he needs to know about."

"Well, if you ARE moving back in, Betsy took over your room, but Trudy's old room is vacant." Larry put his arm around his new bride and squeezed her tightly towards his body.

"What were you thinking, Trudy?"

"Grandy, are you jealous? I know you always had a thing for Larry. But he's all mine." Trudy gazed lovingly into his eyes and batted her near nonexistent eyelashes.

"Yeah, I'm jealous, real jealous. If I was married to Mr. Pervert here, I'd roll him in salt and put him in a barrel of brine." Grandy rolled her eyes and turned to look down the hall. "Let's find Lillian so we can get out of here, Bernie."

"Oh, yeah. Congratulations on your marriage." Bernice tried to be cordial, but felt sorry that Trudy was now sharing a room with the second most disgusting man she knew. Dog Face Dale had the honor of first place.

The ladies found Lillian sitting in the cafeteria, taking a break.

"Hey, you two! What are you doing here?"

"Just stopped by for a visit," Bernice gave Lillian a hug.

"I heard about your accident. How's the leg, Grandy?"

"Getting the cast off today."

"She thinks she's gonna take it off herself. I told her she needs to see the doctor."

"Bernice is right. You really should let the doctor do that."

"Well, my brother's gonna do it for nothing."

Lillian and Bernice smiled at each other, knowing how fruitless it would be to argue with Grandy.

"I'm gonna go wait with Dale. Hurry up your visit, Bernie. We gotta get working on our plan."

"Okay," answered Bernice.

Grandy wheeled herself out to the parking lot as Bernice visited with Lillian.

"I didn't want to say anything in front of Grandy, but I've been thinking about coming back."

"You have? Oh, we'd love to have you, but what about your travels on the road with Grandy?"

"Grandy is in denial. The motor home is totaled. She didn't have enough insurance to replace it and now we're stuck. I was in Texas with my daughter and her family for a while, but I just don't like it there. I'll go back and visit, but I can't continue to live there."

"How about we talk to Irene and get some papers for you to take with you. That way you'll be ahead of the game when you make your final decision."

"Okay. Just don't say anything to anyone, okay, Lillian?"

"Your secret is safe with me. But I have really missed you, Bernice, so I hope you come back."

"It's looking pretty certain, but I'll know more in a day or two."

Chapter 54

Bernice sat between the dysfunctional siblings, trying desperately to hold back her tears. At first it was because of her uncertain future. Was she going to end up back at *Passages of Time*? Would she have to go back to Joyce's? As she chewed on her options, she soon realized her pain also had to do with the uncomfortable ride in Dog Face's pick up. Every bump caused Bernice's head to bang against the gun rack mounted behind her.

"Where to, now?" asked Dale. "Is there anywhere you'd like to go, Miss Bernice? I'm at your service." Dog Face pressed his wide as a coffee table thigh against Bernice.

"Wherever Grandy wants to go." Bernice said. Her demeanor resigned to putting up with whatever Grandy and her brother decided to do.

"We're going to your house Dale, so you can saw this thing off my leg," Grandy commanded.

"Are you sure you shouldn't let – "

"Don't start in, Bernie. Dale's done this before, right, Dale?"

"Not a problem, Sis. I took one off my own arm just a couple of years ago and earlier this spring I removed a cast off Twosome Teddy's torso."

The unusual name of Twosome Teddy caught Bernice's attention and, although she dared not ask, she still did. "A cast from his torso?"

"Yeah, old Teddy had this large hairy growth attached to his chest. Almost looked like another head. He finally had the doctor remove it but there were a few complications and the doc put a cast on him. Teddy got tired of not being able to flop down in his recliner unaided so he had me saw the cast off."

"Is he alright?" asked Bernice.

"He's fine, the saw blade nicked him just a little because he sneezed just as I was almost done."

"See, Grandy, I told you —" Bernice's voice was headed towards the alarm stage.

"Relax Miss Bernice," Dale snorted, "I wouldn't dare hurt Grandy. She'd put my entire body in a cast."

"Damn right," Grandy replied.

Bernice sat quietly with her head turned towards Grandy, trying not to breathe in the homemade cologne Dale was wearing.

"Here we are." Dale grinded the gears on his truck as he turned into his driveway. Bernice coughed as dust blew into the windows. Once the cloud of dust had settled, Bernice surveyed the disaster before her.

Dale's house was an eight foot wide by forty-eight foot long dry van semi trailer with a 10-foot lean-to on one side. The heavy double trailer doors were propped open with cement blocks and there was an eight foot makeshift screen door laying against the opening. The metal frame was bent and the screen had several large holes in it. Bernice could see small portholes had been cut into the semi trailer for windows. Inside the lean-to was a huge mound of split firewood. Weeds and thistles was the extent of the landscaping. Piles of car parts, old refrigerators, washers and dryers lined the driveway and the perimeter of the house and ancient collapsing barn.

"Home sweet home, Miss Bernice. It isn't much but it's cozy." Dale smiled as he gazed upon his place.

Since she could not find a compliment for Dale's place, Bernice asked, "What do you do with all the appliances?"

"I buy them as junk and fix 'em up and sell 'em, good as new."

"Yeah, like old Mrs. Feeney's dryer that caught fire and burned up half her house." Grandy said.

"That wasn't my fault, Sis. That dryer was working just fine when I hooked it up. Old widow Feeney is senile. She thought it was her oven and put all kinds of crap in it. Between eggs, oil and who knows what else, it's no wonder it started on fire."

"Enough about that old broad, get my chair and let's go get this thing off. It's itching worse than poison ivy on the bottom on my feet."

As Dale removed the wheelchair from the back of the truck, Bernice exited the pickup. Her ears immediately picked up on the sound of panting and running. She turned just in time to see Dale's obese Bulldog lurching at her. Bernice barely managed to jump to the side before the mutt could topple her. She took her cane and waved it at the dog yelling, "Go away or I'll hit you!"

Dog Face laughed and said, "Jasper won't hurt ya. He just wants a kiss." The scrubby owner reached down and kissed his look-alike on the mouth, their jowls swaying and slobbering in unison.

"That is so disgusting!" Bernice cringed and held her hand to her mouth.

"What?" Dale held a look of confusion.

"Never mind the dog, let's get this cast off." It was evident Grandy's patience was thinning.

Dale pet Jasper one last time and cooed to him, "Go on now Puppy, Daddy has company."

Jasper turned from Dale and began chasing after a butterfly. The scare from Jasper irritated Bernice's bladder so she suddenly had to pee, real bad. The thought of going into Dale's dark trailer frightened her even more. She imagined there were more germs on his toilet seat than all the world's public toilets put together. There was no way she could wait much longer though. Bernice reluctantly asked Dale, "I need to use a bathroom."

"Sure Honey, the outhouse is right around the corner by the barn." Dale said. "Do you want me to show you?"

"No thank you, I'm sure I can find my way." The sad senior citizen didn't think life could get much worse. "At least I have tissue and moist towelettes in my purse," she thought as she made her way around unrecognizable rusty objects and swatted at biting deer flies.

Surprised to see the exterior of the outhouse in better shape than Dale's house, Bernice was forced to smile at the painted stick figures of men, women and several kinds of animals on the outhouse. Opening the door however, proved to be a near death experience for the bloated-bladdered woman. The stench was so powerful, the faded torn posters of Farrah Fawcett were curling up. Flies buzzed around a rusty coffee can with a roll of dusty toilet paper was stuck in it. Deciding there was no way she could use the facility, Bernice walked behind the outhouse, leaned against it, pulled down here britches and peed outside.

* * * * *

"Here, Miss Bernice, you can sit right here." Dale pulled up a stained, old, upholstered chair with exposed springs towards the woman just walking into the shed.

"That's alright, I'll stand."

Dale began to saw on Grandy's cast.

"You mess up my leg Brother, and I'll send you to Mars in tiny pieces."

"I don't need another reminder Grandy, now just relax."

Bernice turned her head, not wanting to see blood gushing from Grandy's leg. Surprisingly, the cast came off quite smoothly. Grandy's leg had atrophied over the two months of inactivity. She tried to stand on it, but it was too weak to support her weight.

"Does it hurt?" asked Bernice.

"No, it's just fine."

"You might have to go to physical therapy."

"No, I'm not going to physical therapy. A waste of time and money."

"Pew, it smells." Bernice plugged her nose.

"Well, I guess so. It hasn't had a bath in two months." Grandy was gratified as she was finally able to scratch her leg all over. She grabbed a greasy rag, poured turpentine on it and rubbed her leg with it.

"So, where to now?" asked Dale.

"We're gonna have to talk about that," answered Grandy. "The way I see it, if we go back to Avis', they're gonna have me committed."

"So where do you want to go?" asked Bernice.

"I'm goin' back to Avis'. I have to get my things... and..."

"Oh, yeah, Ditch. How's he doin'?" asked Bernice.

"He's anxious to get out on the road. Augusta is teaching him a bunch of stupid tricks and I know he can't stand Lisa, Laney or whatever her name is."

"Now, Grandy, you know we can't go out on the road. We don't have a vehicle." Bernice tried to reason with her stubborn friend once again.

"Everybody keeps telling me that, but I haven't seen my motor home. Dale hasn't seen it, either. What does Bud know about motor homes? If somebody said somebody was dead and you never saw the dead body, how would you really be sure they were dead?"

"You got a point there, Sis."

"Shut up Dale, I think we need to go get my stuff, and Ditch. And then Dale, you can take us to Idaho to assess the damages before we make our final decision on what to do next."

"Now Grandy, I have a job to worry about and Jasper too. I just can't be taking off for who knows how long. Why don't you and Miss Bernice get an apartment or something? Heck, you two could even stay with me. I can take the sleeping bag out of Jasper's doghouse for you and Miss Bernice could sleep on my old army cot in my bedroom."

"And where would you be sleeping?" asked Bernice, fear rapidly curling inside her stomach.

"In my own bed of course, in my bedroom."

Bernice shuttered and replied, "Thanks for the offer, but no thanks."

Grandy agreed, "You have really bad hygiene Brother. Bernie and I would suffocate if we had to be in the same house with you and your T Rex size farts. And we can't get an apartment, Dummy, they're too expensive. Besides, I need to be out on the open road." Grandy paused for a moment before her blue eyes lit up, "Hey! The motorcycles that I won, we could take those Bernie! Buy a sidecar for Ditch, a trailer for our stuff and we'd be all set."

"No way, Grandy! You just got your cast off, your leg's not up to that kind of strain," Bernice insisted.

"I'll tell you what I'm not up for. I'm not up for going back to my daughter-in-law's cooking, and I know I'm not up to going to the loony bin."

"What about *Passages*?"

"Are you nuts?! How could you even think about moving back there, Bernie?"

"I just don't see any other choice."

"Yes there is. Dale, you **are** taking us to see our motor home."

"Yes Grandy." It would be absolutely fruitless to argue with the determined space alien lover, so Dale sighed and shoved his hands in his pant pockets. "So how do we get your stuff without anyone seeing you?"

"Liza and Avis are both at work, Augusta's at school."

"What about the maid, the one who answered the phone?" asked Bernice.

"I'll let Dale distract her while you and I go gather my things. What's she gonna do, anyway, call Avis? By the time he gets there, we'll be long gone."

Dale began grabbing stuff from the shed shelves and tossing it into a five-gallon paint bucket. "This should be enough to distract the maid," he beamed.

Grandy wheeled herself out to the pickup while Bernice followed her.

"I'll go with you to the house, but I won't be going to Idaho with you."

"Why not?" Grandy said tersely.

"Because I - " Bernice was too much of a lady to say it in front of Dale, but pretty much the only reason she didn't want to go was because she knew her stomach couldn't take sitting next to Dale for one more mile, let alone several hundred. "Because I think the pickup would be too crowded with three adults and two dogs."

"That's a stupid reason, Bernie. You and the dogs can ride in the back. Dale has a topper we can put on the truck so you don't get wet if it rains."

Chapter 55

Under the pretense that a bottle of Crown Royal whiskey was given to him as a gift from a distributor, Howard set the bottle and two glasses on the kitchen table in front of Lester.

"Looky here Dad, we can drink in style tonight," Howard said as he poured the first of several glasses for his father. The old man tossed the first two ounces down his throat before his son had a chance to bring the bottle close to his own glass. Howard hoped it wasn't going to take more than one bottle of the expensive liquor to seduce Lester into a long, deep sleep.

For the second round, the two men clinked their glasses together as Lester made a toast. "Here's to the man who created this golden smooth nectar and to the woman who drove me to drinking it, your mother."

"To Mom," said Howard, not feeling at all the same way about her that his father did. Sometime later that night, the youngest son convinced Lester they should continue their celebrating in the livingroom. Pretending to be much more wasted than he was, Howard kept debating his father on various issues so he wouldn't keep track of how much he wasn't drinking. The Crown Royal bottle was nearly empty when Howard was relieved to see his dad finally pass out on the couch. He left the old man snoring and drooling as he quietly went to his bedroom and slid in bed next to his wife.

"Are yo ready for tomorrow?" Blackie whispered.

"As ready as I'll ever be."

* * * * *

Dakota glanced at his watch for the fourth time in five minutes. It was past noon and Howard was fifteen minutes late. The afternoon air was a comfortable 72 degrees as he sat at a cement picnic table outside a fast food restaurant. Dakota's mind kept running from subject to subject, much like a baseball player making his way around a baseball diamond. The first issue had to do with his conversation with Howard. Dakota believed his sibling would be right beside him when he went to see his mother. But swirling around in Dakota's brain was also a small sliver of fear that Lester may have found out about the meeting or Howard might have changed his mind or that even Avis had been tipped off about their plans.

The next base had to do with his mother. Was the plan to move her to an apartment near Howard going to work? How could he and his brother really keep Lester from finding out where she was? At this point in the game, the middle son knew he and Howard had prepared as best they could for their mother's future.

Then a third softer and sweeter thought entered Dakota's brain. It was of his wife Skye and their young son Rain. At least there was peace knowing the two of them were enjoying a day at the Science Museum.

Just as Dakota was checking his watch again, Howard drove up in his red Toyota pickup. He exited the vehicle and the brothers shook hands. They noticed the weight changes, new stress lines and weariness in each other.

"Good to see you Howard," Dakota said with sincerity.

"Same here," Howard replied, "Sorry I'm late, had a little trouble with my last beer delivery."

"That's okay. We still staying with the plan we talked about?"

"Yeah, we just show up during the day when no one else is home and take Mom out of the place."

"Is anybody there helping her out during the day?"

"Consuelo, Avis' maid is there."

"Will she be a problem?" Concern etched on Dakota's face.

"Not sure about that one. That's a bridge we'll cross when we get there. Let's get some lunch and we can go over our plan once more.

Dakota and Howard headed towards Denny's in their respective vehicles.

* * * * *

Accustomed to hangovers, Lester woke to face a room that looked fuzzy along with buzzing sounds in his ears. Tossing the sheet that had covered his sweaty body to the side, Lester rolled off the couch and staggered into the kitchen. Opening the refrigerator door, he scanned the shelves for his cure to feeling out of sync. He found a beer and guzzled it down in 7 seconds. The world immediately started to come into focus and he looked for something to eat. Seeing a container of pastries on the counter, Lester continually stuffed them into his mouth until he had eaten eight of the nine donuts in the box. White powdered sugar, chocolate and sprinkles circled his mouth. Crumbs tumbled onto his dirty sleeveless T-shirt and fell onto the kitchen floor. For lack of what to do next, the old man grabbed the remaining donut and went back to the livingroom. Thinking Howard was at work and Blackie was still sleeping, he turned on the T.V. and watched two hours of soap operas. When it was noon and there was no sign of Blackie, Lester wandered down the hallway to her and Howard's bedroom. Their door stood open and the bed had been made.

Confusion was now heating up in Lester and he called Howard's cell phone. It went directly to voice mail so he tried it again, and again. He didn't have Blackie's cell phone number so he began digging around in drawers hoping he would find it. What he did find, besides a man and woman's private objects, was a small notepad in the night stand drawer next to their bed. The top page was blank but showed indentation marks. Lester snooped until he found a pencil. He rub the lead across the tablet until he could make out the words, "noon, Paul." For several minutes the old man kept mumbling "Paul" to himself. Who is Paul? Is he Howard's friend or maybe Blackie's friend?

When one o'clock came and went and there was no sign of Blackie, Lester dialed Howard's cell phone and left a rambling message about a Paul and Blackie. He went back into the kitchen, drank another beer, ate a package of baloney swimming in horseradish.

Just as Lester was contemplating his next move, Blackie drove into the driveway. She exited her car with several bags in her arms. Once inside the house, she noticed Lester staring at her.

"What's wrong with you?" she said with no emotion.

"Nothing. Where you been all day?"

"None of your business."

"It is my business if it concerns my son. Who is Paul?" Demanded Lester.

"Paul? What are you talking about?"

"I saw the note that said noon, Paul on your night stand. Are you out fooling around on Howard?"

"Are you nuts? I'd never cheat on Howard. And what are you doing in our bedroom anyway, you pervert."

"So who is Paul?"

"It's St. Paul, you idiot."

"Well then, who's in St. Paul?"

"None of your business, Lester."

A strange look came over the old man's face and he said to Blackie, "I'll bring in the rest of your bags."

"I can get them just fine myself."

"No please I insist," and Lester headed out the door.

"You don't have any shoes on."

"That's okay, I'll be fine." Lester hurried to the small sedan, jumped in and took off. He had figured out what was in St. Paul, Minnesota.

Chapter 56

On the ride back to Avis', Grandy and Bernice talked about formulating a concrete plan for their future. Bernice reminded Grandy that her sister Charlotte had given them each $2,500 and maybe the best thing to do was rent an apartment together. The feisty redhead disagreed and felt the money should go towards repairs on the motor home.

Bernice sounded exasperated as she said, "Grandy, let's just get your things from Avis', go stay a couple of days at my hotel room and then decide."

"Fine – "

"What about me?" Dog Face butted in, "Do I get to stay with you, too?"

"No," the women shouted in unison.

"Well, that's – "

"This doesn't concern you, Dog Face. Just shut your jowls for now," Grandy said firmly, "and follow my instructions."

"Is it going to be a problem getting in and out of Avis' house again?" Bernice asked.

"No. Here's the plan; Dog Face, you drive into the side yard and go ring the door bell at the front door. When Consuelo answers, try to distract her with some story about a missing something. And don't slobber on her. Bernie and I will go through the back door, get Ditch and my stuff and meet you back at your pickup."

As the conspiring threesome turned the corner to Avis' house, Bernice exclaimed, "Look at all those cars! I wonder who's having a party."

Grandy's face went pale and she hollered, "Turn around, now! Most of those vehicles are parked by Avis'. He's probably got all kinds of lawyer buddies, private detectives and bounty hunters after me. Turn around, Dog Face!"

"I can't, Sis, there's a red pickup behind me and the street isn't wide enough to make a U-turn."

Bernice squinted her eyes then said, "Wait a minute! There's my sister Charlotte!"

"What's she doing here?" Grandy demanded, "Is she part of a scheme to put me away?"

"How can you say that, Grandy?" Bernice asked in surprise. "Charlotte is not that kind of person and you know that! Now stop the truck next to her, I'll find out what is going on."

Dale pulled up next to Charlotte and a large crowd collected next to her. As soon as Bernice got out of the truck, people she didn't recognize came towards her. Bernice and Charlotte rushed to each other for a warm sisterly hug.

"Charlotte, what are you doing here? What are all these other people doing here?"

"We're here for yours and Grandy's big surprise."

"Surprise? What kind of surprise?"

"You'll find out in just a little bit." Charlotte's face beamed as she thought about what was in store for her sister and her friend.

Bernice glanced around, "Is Henry here, too?"

"No, we parted ways two days ago. It's a long story and I'll tell you about it later. But because I had so much fun traveling in a motor home with you and Grandy, I rented that small Winnebago. See." Charlotte pointed across the street.

As Grandy watched the reunion between Bernice and Charlotte, Dakota poked his head in the passenger window while Howard stuck his face in the driver's side window.

"Hi, Ma!" the two brothers said in unison.

"Holy crap!" Dog Face yelled as he and Grandy jumped in their seats.

"What the -- ?" said the redhead as she opened her door to get out. Her sons quickly embraced their mother with loving hugs.

"What are you doing here? Are you part of this huge group of people?" Grandy asked.

"No, we were just wondering what was going on ourselves," said Dakota, "Howard and I were coming to get you from Avis' and set you up in an apartment near his place."

"Thanks for the offer, Boys, but Bernie and I are going to spend a couple of days at her hotel room and design our own plans."

"Are you sure, Ma?" Howard said with concern.

"Of course I'm sure. Now you boys get my wheelchair from the back of the pick-up so we can find out what the heck is going on with Bernie and Charlie."

Howard, Dakota, Grandy and Dog Face all made their way to where Bernice and Charlotte were still in deep conversation. The people who were coming closer to Grandy and Bernice were smiling and waving at the two friends.

"What's going on?" Grandy demanded, "Why are all these people here?"

"Charlotte says there is a big surprise waiting for us by Avis' house," Bernice said.

"Does this surprise include Avis and men in white coats?" Suspicion was evident in Grandy's voice.

Just as Grandy was considering turning around and going back to her brother's pickup, the crowd parted and Chet Baxter walked up to the small huddled group.

"Chet?" Bernice exclaimed.

"Yup, it's me." He looked at Grandy and said, "Come on Grandy, there is a wonderful surprise waiting for you and Bernice."

"That's what people keep telling us, what the heck is going on?" Grandy insisted.

"All these people are members of your fan club, Grandy. They have traveled from all over the United States to come and present you and Bernice with a present," explained Chet.

Familiar faces began to appear along the sidewalk as the traveling grandmas made their way to Avis' circular driveway.

There was Tina and Toni, the hairdressers from Winnemucca, Nevada, Bud and Flossy from Idaho, Tom from Reno, Nevada and a huge group of Red Hat Society members all hooting and hollering.

When Grandy and Bernice reached the front of Avis's house, a brand new Fleetwood motor home sat in the driveway. From behind another large group of fans, many of them from the ISAET organization, Roscoe came forth and handed Grandy a set of keys.

"This is for you, Grandy and Bernice," he said kindly. "Your fans pooled together their resources and bought you a new coach so you could get back on the road again."

The two women were speechless. Bernice began fanning herself so she wouldn't hyperventilate and Grandy got up out of her purple wheelchair and walked towards her new vehicle. Her sons kept close to her side, making sure she wouldn't fall down. They also keeping a watchful eye out for their older brother.

"How did you keep this such a surprise?" Bernice managed to ask.

A light chuckle from Chet preceded his answer. "After receiving dozens of calls from people wondering how they could help you after your accident, I decided to set up a special fund for the purpose of buying you a new motor home. I thought it would take quite a while to get enough to buy one, but apparently you have more adoring fans than I thought. It didn't take any time at all for there people to accumulate enough money to purchase the vehicle. Taxes, license and full insurance coverage has also been taken care of. We asked each donor to keep quiet about the plan to surprise you with it. Pretty much everyone knew that you wouldn't want your son Avis or your ex husband Lester to know about it. We weren't sure what to do when we found out you were staying with the very person you were trying to avoid. But after talking to Bernice's daughter Joyce, we figured we would go ahead with the plans to present it to you wherever you were."

Bernice's grey eyes widened at the mention of her daughter. "You mean Joyce knew all about this?"

"Yes, she did."

"But she never let on one bit. In fact she acted like my trip to Minnesota wasn't the best idea," Bernice shook her head when she thought about her conversations with her daughter.

A familiar dog bark reached Grandy's eyes just as she was about to enter the motor home. Ditch came running out of the house with Augusta hot on his heels. The mutt ran straight to his owner and she scooped him up.

"What are you doing home?" Grandy asked her granddaughter, "You're supposed to be in school."

"I'm playing hooky so I could be here when all these people showed up."

"You knew about this, too?"

"Yes, Grandma, I even sent in my allowance for three weeks to help pay for the motor home."

Grandy grunted and ruffled Augusta's pin-striped hair. "I suppose you expect me to give you a ride in my new Fleetwood?"

"Yes I do."

"What if I don't want to?"

"Then I'll blackmail you just like I did Consuelo. I told her if she called Mom or Dad and told them about today that I would make sure she got blamed for drinking Dad's expensive wine."

Grandy stared at her pint sized relative and looked to her sons for help. "Augusta, go say hi to your uncles before I get on the radio and tell everyone in this country that you kiss a poster of the Hanson brothers every night."

Augusta reluctantly visited with Dakota and Howard as Grandy and Bernice shook hands, hugged and thanked all the people who had showed up for their surprise. Dog Face continued to keep an eye out for Avis. Charlotte waltzed into Avis' house and told Consuelo she was packing up Grandy's belongings and taking them out to the motor home. The house maid said nothing and returned to the kitchen to start supper.

It was a solid forty-five minutes later when the traveling roommates finished their acknowledgments. Grandy had become increasingly crabby as time wore on and she finally sat down in her wheelchair and pushed herself to the steps of the motor home.

"I'm ready to go now, Bernie," she said loudly.

"Once you're settled in, don't forget to call us and tell us about your new adventures," Chet said with enthusiasm,. "It should be obvious there are a lot of people who love you."

"Ma, don't keep turning your cell phone off, we want to be able to get a hold of you," Dakota said.

"I wouldn't mind chatting with you once in awhile, too," Roscoe added.

"Bye, Grandma," Augusta shouted.

"Yeah, yeah," Grandy replied as she started the motor home. "Bernie, buckle in, we're headed for Canada."

"But Grandy, we need passports to go there."

"Not the route I'm taking."

"I don't have any of my things. What am I supposed to wear for clothing and my makeup is back at the hotel." Bernice was starting to get in her whiney mode.

"I'll share my stuff until we can go shopping."

"What about my things, though?"

"I'll send Dog Face to the hotel; he can tell them he's your husband and get your belongings."

Bernice sighed and mumbled, "If you send your brother to get my stuff you might as well have him burn all of it. I can't imagine anything more disgusting than having him touch my underwear."

* * * * *

Just as Grandy and Bernice's new Fleetwood was exiting Avis' driveway, Blackie's sedan driven by Lester entered the street at a high rate of speed. He almost hit the motor home but swerved at the last minute, side swiping a mailbox when he saw who was driving the vehicle. Lester was being pursued by three police cars with lights flashing and sirens at highest pitch. From the opposite direction, Avis was rubbernecking from his car all the retreating vehicles from around his place. Too obsessed with the scenes around them, Avis and Lester realized too late the consequence of their inattentiveness. The sound of blaring horns and smashing fenders echoed up and down the block. Father and son looked at each other in a fury through cracked windshields. Before the duo could engage in a shouting match, a brand new Fleetwood motor home cruised past them. The wild, redheaded driver smiled and waved to her greedy son and loser ex-husband.

* * * * *

About the Authors

Dona was born and raised in St. Helena, California, in the beautiful Napa Valley. In 1974, she married Bob Bakker, her childhood sweetheart. They settled in Napa and raised their two children, Heather and Jay, now ages 32 and 27, respectively.

Since 1976, Dona has owned and operated her home-based secretarial business, providing services to doctors, lawyers, small business owners and individuals in the Napa area. During the course of her business, she has typed and/or edited numerous books for local authors. It was through these assignments that she realized she had a story of her own and began writing her first book. In *Run of the Mill - A True Life, Napa Valley Adventure*, which was published in 2004, Dona recalls five years of her childhood growing up in St. Helena with her brother and their grandparents, who were caretakers of The Old Bale Mill, an historical monument built in the mid-1800s.

A year later, Dona co-wrote her first novel with her longtime friend, Tami Riedeman, who resides in Sandstone, Minnesota. Tami and Dona met in church over 20 years ago and, even though they no longer live in the same town, their love of the Lord and their sense of humor has kept their friendship alive. They worked so well together and had so much fun writing *The Golden Road, French Wine or Moonshine?* that they continued the story in this sequel, *The Golden Road Detour.* Through their writing together, their friendship has grown even stronger, in spite of the many miles between them.

In 2008, Dona also co-wrote *St. Helena High School, Circa 1940-1972, The Golden Years - An Age of Maturity and Achievement* with 97 year old Ralph Ingols, retired teacher/counselor. The book is a tribute to the 2000+ students who passed through the halls of St. Helena High School during Ralph Ingols' tenure there.

Over the years, Dona has served as Mother Advisor for St. Helena Rainbow, Brownie and Girl Scout Leader. She has been involved in various ministries through her church, including rest home visitation, children's ministries such as AWANA leader (Approved Workmen Are Not Ashamed), and she served as Area Coordinator for the Napa Chapter of MITI (Moms In Touch International), which is comprised of groups of moms gathering each week to pray for their children and their particular schools.

In addition to writing, Dona enjoys cycling and hiking in and around the Napa Valley. After 50+ years, she still finds solace in the wondrous beauty of this very special place, and feels blessed to call it her home.

* * * * *

Tami was born in Minnesota and, after living in California, Oregon and Montana, she finally made her way back to her beloved homeland, currently residing in Sandstone, Minnesota.

Tami has two children, Justin 23 and Becky 21. She and her husband David have been married six years and live on a beautiful hobby ranch that they have named KoodB Ranch. Since there are no two-legged young ones to spoil, Tami and David heap lots of attention on their horses, cats and dog. David is an owner/operator truck driver and Tami works two jobs, her favorite being an ad sales/composition position at the Hinckley Newspaper.

Ever since Tami was introduced to a poetry course in the fifth grade, she has developed a passion for putting words together. During her adolescence and young adulthood, creating poetry chapbooks became her first introduction into the publishing world. Tami entered contests, taught a poetry unit at an elementary school, formed writer's groups and added short stories and novels to her writing experiences.

Dona and Tami's friendship is a true testament to how people can learn from each other and endure despite completely opposite lifestyles. Where Dona is city, Tami is country. Co-writing two books together has been a wild, fun-filled ride neither one will ever forget and both hope to continue in the future.

Besides being co-author of *The Golden Road, French Wine or Moonshine?* and *The Golden Road Detour*, Tami has two other books in the works as well as writing a bi-weekly humorous column for the Hinckley Newspaper.

Tami's interests and hobbies are not limited to writing. Photography is another pastime that has also brought her into the publishing world. Two of her photos, one for a magazine and one for a book, are in the lineup to be printed in the next few months. A well-known magazine called "Country" is also featuring Tami, David and their hobby farm in the April/May 2009 issue.

In Tami's pockets of spare time, she trains and rides horses, does scrap booking and creates quilts. More importantly though, she prefers her time be spent with God, David and her friends and family.

Acknowledgments

First and foremost, thank you to our Lord, Jesus Christ, for bringing us together and keeping our friendship strong through all of life's peaks and valleys; for the joy and laughter we shared while "working" on this book.

Tami is always grateful for the immense support and input from her husband David. He continues to fill her life with laughter, adventure and love. His patience is immeasurable, especially when it comes to Tami's passion for pets.

Everyday the love Tami has for her children grows. Without Justin and Becky, it would be a dark world. There is also much appreciation for Tami's parents, David and Bonnie Krinke and David's parents, Mike and Jan Riedeman. Their encouragement is backbone to Tami's pursuit of her ventures.

Dona thanks her husband, Bob, for choosing her to be his Queen for life and for his never ending love and support.

Dona is grateful for the privilege of raising her two children, Heather and Jay, which has afforded her an abundance of inspiration for her writing.

To Neil Magnuson, thank you once again for your honest assessment of our manuscript. We appreciate it.

Lauana Nelson, we thank you for capturing our imagination through your artwork.

Thank you to all of our friends and family, too numerous to mention here by name, who shared their ideas along the journey.

Thanks to all who read our first book, for their enthusiasm and encouragement to keep going with this sequel.

Thank you to the many media outlets, stores, groups and retirement homes for their assistance in our marketing efforts with *The Golden Road, French Wine or Moonshine?* We look forward to continuing that relationship.

Thank you to the many sassy seniors in our lives, past and present, who inspired our colorful characters.

ORDERING INFORMATION

Copies of *The Golden Road - French Wine or Moonshine?*
and *The Golden Road Detour* available as follows:

Pastime Publications
1370 Trancas Street, #372
Napa, CA 94558
(707) 252-4062
www.napavalleypastime.com

or

KoodB Creations
P.O. Box 614
Sandstone, MN 55072
(320) 245-6949
koodbwriting.com